“What t

wit

The slick-haired professor at the piano abruptly stopped playing, and most of the rest of the noise in the room died away as well. Longarm turned his head slowly and saw a huge man standing a few feet away. Behind him was a clear path all the way to the batwing doors of the saloon, which were still gently swinging back and forth. Longarm knew from the evidence that the big gent had just come in—and folks had gotten out of his way in a hurry.

“You jawing at me, friend?” asked Longarm in a deceptively mild voice.

“Damn right,” rumbled the man, who probably topped out at six inches over six feet. “Damn right I’m talkin’ to you, you short-growed little runt. Get your damn hand off Anna Marie.”

“If the lady wants me to let go of her, I reckon she’ll tell me so,” Longarm pointed out reasonably.

The big stranger cuffed his sombrero back so it hung from the chin strap looped around his thick neck. “Looks like I’m gonna have to teach you some manners, mister,” he growled.

DON'T MISS THESE
ALL-ACTION WESTERN SERIES
FROM THE BERKLEY PUBLISHING GROUP

THE GUNSMITH by J. R. Roberts
Clint Adams was a legend among lawmen, outlaws, and ladies. They called him . . . the Gunsmith.

LONGARM by Tabor Evans
The popular long-running series about U.S. Deputy Marshal Long—his life, his loves, his fight for justice.

SLOCUM by Jake Logan
Today's longest-running action Western. John Slocum rides a deadly trail of hot blood and cold steel.

BUSHWHACKERS by B. J. Lanagan
An all-new series by the creators of Longarm! The rousing adventures of the most brutal gang of cutthroats ever assembled—Quantrill's Raiders.

TABOR EVANS
LONGARM
AND THE
BORDER WILDCAT

JOVE BOOKS, NEW YORK

LONGARM AND THE BORDER WILDCAT

A Jove Book / published by arrangement with
the author

PRINTING HISTORY
Jove edition / January 1998

The Putnam Berkley World Wide Web site address is
http://www.berkley.com

ISBN: 0-515-12209-2

A JOVE BOOK®
Jove Books are published by The Berkley Publishing Group, a member
of Penguin Putnam Inc.,
200 Madison Avenue, New York, New York 10016.
JOVE and the "J" design are trademarks
belonging to Jove Publications, Inc.

PRINTED IN THE UNITED STATES OF AMERICA

10 9 8 7 6 5 4 3 2 1

LONGARM
AND THE
BORDER WILDCAT

Chapter 1

The beautiful redhead squirmed on Longarm's lap as he drew her head down to his and kissed her. Her lips parted eagerly, and before his tongue had a chance to slide into her mouth, her tongue was exploring his. At the same time, she dropped her hand to his groin and began massaging his rapidly hardening shaft.

Longarm broke the kiss and said in a husky voice, "I hate to tell you to stop what you're doing, darlin', but we *are* in a public place."

"No one here will care," she told him as her fingers tightened on him.

That was true. Nobody else in this Del Rio saloon seemed to be paying any attention at all to what was going on at the table in the back corner of the room. They were too busy laughing and talking and drinking and gambling and doing plenty of carousing of their own.

Longarm sighed. "I reckon you're right. But I'd still feel a mite more comfortable upstairs in your room."

She gave his manhood a final squeeze. "All right, Custis, if that is what you wish. Come."

That was just what he intended to do in a little while, Longarm thought wryly as the redhead took his hand and led him toward the staircase. Other patrons of the place had been trooping up and down the stairs all evening with the rest of the girls who worked there, but the redhead had been concentrating on Longarm alone ever since he'd come in. He didn't know whether to feel flattered . . .

Or suspicious.

After all, he *was* here in Del Rio on business. He wasn't advertising the fact that he was a United States deputy marshal, but it was no secret either. This assignment wasn't an undercover job at all—even though under the covers was where he figured to be pretty soon.

Or on top of them anyway. It was too hot here in this Texas border country to be burrowing down under the sheets. A fella needed all the night breeze he could get.

The redhead's fingers clenched on his with surprising strength as they neared the bottom of the staircase. She stopped and caught her breath. Longarm nearly bumped into her. He asked, "What's the matter"—then paused, trying to remember her name—"Anna Marie?"

Instead of the redhead's sultry voice, furious tones that resembled the roar of a grizzly bear provided the answer to Longarm's question. "What the *hell* are you doin' with my woman?"

The slick-haired professor at the piano abruptly stopped playing, and most of the rest of the noise in the room died away as well. Longarm turned his head slowly and saw a huge man standing a few feet away. Behind him was a clear path all the way to the bat-wing doors of the saloon, which were still swinging gently back and forth. Longarm knew from that evidence that the big gent had just come in—and folks had gotten out of his way in a hurry.

"You jawing at me, friend?" asked Longarm in a deceptively mild voice.

"Damn right," rumbled the man, who probably topped out at six inches over six feet. "Damn right I'm talkin' to you, you short-growed little runt. Get your damn hand offa Anna Marie."

Longarm didn't much appreciate being called a runt, since he was well over six feet himself. Since it was his left hand that the redheaded saloon girl was holding so tightly, he made no effort to disengage it. His right could still reach for the Colt snugly holstered in the cross-draw rig at his waist if need be.

"If the lady wants me to let go of her, I reckon she'll tell me so," Longarm pointed out reasonably. As he had suspected, though, the burly bearded stranger was in no mood to be reasonable.

The big man was wearing a sombrero, which made him look even taller, but he wasn't Mexican despite his swarthy complexion and short dark beard. The muscles of his arms and shoulders strained against a butternut shirt and a black and white cowhide vest. He wore denim trousers tucked into soft leather boots with high fringed tops. The leather-wrapped hilt of what appeared to be a Bowie knife stuck up from the top of the right boot. A gunbelt was strapped around his waist, with a long-barreled, pearl-handled Remington revolver in the holster. He looked like a formidable hombre, thought Longarm.

But the federal star-packer was no shrinking violet himself. Tall and rangy, he wore a flat-crowned, snuff-brown Stetson and the pants and vest from a brown tweed suit; because of the heat, he had left the coat in his hotel room. His white shirt was still fairly crisp, and the string tie around his neck was expertly knotted. Some folks might consider the outfit to be that of a fancy dude, but one look at Longarm's rugged, mustachioed features, tanned to the color of old saddle leather and weathered by years of exposure to sun and wind and rain, told a different story. So did the ease with which he wore his gun.

The big stranger cuffed the sombrero back so that it hung from the chin strap looped around his thick neck. "Looks like I'm goin' to have to teach you some manners, mister," he growled.

Longarm glanced at the redhead. She was pretty, especially for a woman in a profession which aged its practitioners rapidly, and the breasts that were practically spilling out of her dress looked soft and creamy and were dotted with tiny freckles. He could imagine plunging his face between those globes of flesh and gleefully wallowing there for a while . . . but would the experience be worth a knock-down-drag-out fight with this bruiser of a Texan?

Probably not, Longarm decided. Besides, he was here in Del Rio to work, not to brawl. The assignment would get under way the next morning, and he wanted to be well rested for it.

All that was really left to consider was his honor, and Longarm decided that it hadn't been mortally wounded yet. He could afford to be magnanimous about the whole thing.

"I didn't come here looking for trouble," he said as he let go of Anna Marie's hand. "I just wanted a drink before I turned in, so I reckon that's what I'll have." He started to turn away, intending to head back to the table in the corner.

"Haw!" The explosive bark of laughter came from the big man. "I knew that fella would take water. Come on, you damn redheaded slut. I'm in the mood for some lovin'."

"Leave me alone," snapped Anna Marie. "You are no gentleman, Lazarus Coffin!"

The odd name would have caught Longarm's attention even if Anna Marie hadn't upped and screamed right after saying it. He glanced over his shoulder and saw that the big man had hold of her wrist in what looked like a painfully tight grip as he tried to drag her toward the stairs. Anna Marie was hanging back like a balky mule, but she was no match for Coffin's strength, and no one else in the room was making a move to help her. He hauled her onto the stairs.

Longarm sighed. Looked like things weren't going to be settled peaceably after all.

"Coffin!" he said, his voice ripping through the uneasy silence that still ruled the room. "Let go of her."

Coffin stopped on the third step and frowned ominously. "You buttin' in again, mister? Thought I'd told you to run along like a good li'l feller."

Longarm walked steadily toward the staircase. "I said let her go. You can say what you want about me, but you ain't going to mistreat a lady while I'm around."

"Lady?" Coffin repeated, then gave a braying laugh. "This ain't no lady. This is just a worn-out old whore."

Not hardly, thought Longarm. Anna Marie was a long way from that. As if to prove it, she gasped in anger at Coffin's words and reached up to slap him across the face.

He blinked, more surprised than hurt by the blow. Then his bearded face contorted in an ugly scowl. He raised a hamlike hand to swat her in return.

Longarm palmed the Colt out smoothly and eared back the hammer as he raised the gun and lined the sights on Coffin's broad chest. "I wouldn't," he said quietly.

Coffin's face flushed an even darker shade of red as anger shook him. With a visible effort, he controlled his rage and said, "You don't know what you're doin', mister. You'd better put that gun up and get the hell outta here whilst you still can."

"I ain't going to tell you again," said Longarm. "Let go of the woman."

With a grimace, Coffin released Anna Marie. She stepped back and rubbed her wrist, which bore the marks of Coffin's fingers. Then she spat on his boots before turning and rushing across the saloon to a door at the end of the bar. She disappeared through it.

"All right," said Longarm as he lowered the hammer of his Colt and replaced the weapon in its holster. "It's all over now."

"The hell it is!" Lazarus Coffin stepped down from the staircase and started toward Longarm. One of the poker tables was in his way, so he grasped it and flung it aside as if it was no more than a piece of kindling. Chips and cards flew every which way, and the men who had been sitting at the table sprawled on the sawdust-littered floor as they flung themselves from their chairs and tried to get out of Coffin's way.

Longarm tried being reasonable one last time. "No need for any more trouble," he said with a shake of his head.

Coffin was in range now. He spat an obscene epithet at Longarm and swung a roundhouse punch at the lawman's head.

The blow might have taken Longarm's head off if it had connected, but despite the obvious power in Coffin's body, the man was slow. Longarm ducked under the punch easily. He stepped in and hammered a punch into Coffin's midsection, hoping to end the fight quickly. He hadn't wanted this trouble in the first place.

Longarm winced as his fist connected with Coffin's belly. It was almost like punching a wall. Coffin grunted, just enough to let Longarm know that he had felt the punch, but other than that it didn't seem to have any effect. And Longarm was close enough so that he couldn't get out of the way as Coffin swept him into a bear hug.

Son of a bitch! thought Longarm. This was just about the worst possible thing that could have happened. Coffin's arms closed around him with overpowering strength. Luckily, Longarm had sensed what was about to happen and had quickly caught a deep breath even as Coffin was grabbing him. He had enough air in his lungs to last for a few moments.

Long enough, anyway, for him to lower his head and butt Coffin in the nose. Coffin grunted again and stumbled back a couple of steps. Longarm took advantage of the opportunity to thrust a booted foot between Coffin's ankles. Coffin tripped and swayed backward, trying desperately to hang on to Longarm and keep his balance at the same time. It was a losing proposition. He fell to the floor with a crash, Longarm landing on top of him.

The impact loosened Coffin's grip enough for Longarm to tear his right arm free. He slammed his fist into Coffin's jaw, making the bigger man's head bounce off the planks of the floor. Longarm was about to strike again when Coffin arched his back and with a furious roar flung Longarm off to the side.

Longarm rolled over a couple of times when he landed, then came up quickly on his hands and knees. Everyone else in the saloon had backed off to the edges of the room, giving the combatants plenty of room. Quite a few of the spectators were shouting encouragement, and Longarm judged them to be divided about equally in their support. It was no surprise that Coffin wasn't an overwhelming favorite, even though Longarm was a stranger in Del Rio. He figured that Coffin had been running roughshod over folks around there, so that some of them would be glad to see him get his comeuppance.

Longarm just wished he could guarantee that was the way the fight was going to turn out.

Coffin lunged at him again just as Longarm regained his feet. For a long moment, the two men stood there toe to toe, trading punches, each of them absorbing the punishment dealt out by the other. Longarm knew he couldn't win the fight by this means, but at least he was softening Coffin up a little, he told himself. He tried not to think about the damage Coffin might be doing to him.

Gradually, while they were slugging each other, Longarm worked his way around so that Coffin's back was turned toward the bar. Then, ducking a punch, Longarm threw himself forward and wrapped his arms around Coffin. Taken by surprise, Coffin was forced backward by Longarm's charge. Summoning up all his remaining strength, Longarm rammed Coffin into the bar, bending him back over the hardwood. Coffin roared in pain and rage.

Longarm straightened and landed an uppercut that rocked Coffin's head back even more. The man's throat was exposed below the dark beard, and Longarm chopped at it with the edge of his hand. Coffin gagged and grabbed at his throat. Longarm stepped back to give himself some room, then threw a left and a right that both landed cleanly, snapping Coffin's head from side to side. Longarm hooked another punch to Coffin's belly, and this time his fist sunk satisfyingly in the man's midsection. Coffin doubled over. Longarm clubbed his hands together and brought them sledging down on the back of Coffin's neck.

Coffin fell, and the floor shivered under Longarm's feet from the weight of the big man landing so hard on it. Longarm stepped back and dragged a deep breath into his lungs. Practically every muscle in his body was beginning to ache already, and there was a fluttering of exhaustion deep inside him. He had come close, too damn close, to losing this fight.

A groan came from Coffin's bloodied lips. He tried to push himself up from the floor, failed, and slumped back onto the sawdust-covered planks. All the fight was out of him now.

Movement from the end of the bar caught Longarm's eye. He looked in that direction and saw Anna Marie peering out through the door, which she had opened a few inches. Longarm raised a hand and crooked a finger, summoning her back out into the main room of the saloon. He leaned over and caught hold of Coffin's shirt collar with one hand and the man's belt with the other. With a groan, Longarm hauled Coffin back onto his feet.

Coffin blinked bleary eyes and shook his head, obviously trying to clear away some of the cobwebs that the pounding had left clogging his brain. Longarm gave him a shove that sent him stumbling toward Anna Marie, who drew back in fright.

"Apologize to the lady," rasped Longarm as he grabbed Coffin's arm. "Tell her you're sorry you said those things to her."

Ponderously, Coffin shook his head again. "Ain't goin' to do it," he rumbled.

Longarm drew his gun and pressed the barrel into Coffin's ribs. "The hell you ain't. I said apologize, and that's what you're going to do."

Coffin glared at him, murder shining in his dark eyes, but finally the man turned his shaggy head toward Anna Marie and mumbled, "Reckon I'm sorry."

"Ma'am," Longarm prodded.

"Reckon I'm sorry . . . ma'am," said Coffin. He snarled at Longarm. "There! You satisfied, you bastard?"

"You push your luck a mite for a man who's got a gun barrel tickling his ribs," Longarm said. "But I reckon if the lady's satisfied, I am too." He looked to Anna Marie for confirmation, and she nodded shakily. Longarm let go of Coffin's arm, but not before pushing him against the bar again. Longarm stepped back and holstered his gun.

Coffin reached behind him and pulled his sombrero around where he could see it. He had fallen on top of the hat, and its high-peaked crown was crushed beyond repair. "Aw, hell," he said. "Look what you did."

"You brought it on yourself," Longarm told him. "I said all along I didn't come in here looking for trouble." His own hat had been knocked off in the ruckus, and he looked around for it on the floor. He spotted it and bent over to pick it up.

"Well, you got trouble, all right," said Coffin, his voice a little stronger now. "You got more trouble than you ever dreamed of, mister."

Longarm heard the metallic click of a gun being cocked and tensed, ready to spin around and fling the hat in his hand toward Coffin in the hope that it would distract the man long enough for Longarm to draw his own gun. Coffin's next words stopped him before he could make a move, however.

"You're under arrest," said the big man.

Longarm blinked in surprise and looked back over his shoulder. "Under arrest?" he repeated.

Coffin had the Remington lined on Longarm's back. "That's right," he said. "The charge is disturbin' the peace and assaultin' an officer o' the law. You're goin' to be mighty familiar with the inside of the local hoosegow 'fore you get out, mister . . . what is your name anyway?"

Longarm had to hold back a laugh. "It's Long," he told Coffin, "Custis Long. You trying to tell me you're a lawman, Coffin?"

The gun in Coffin's right hand didn't budge as he moved aside the cowhide vest with his left. Pinned to the pocket of the butternut shirt was a badge, all right. In fact, Longarm recognized it.

It was the famous silver star set in a silver circle. The emblem of the Texas Rangers.

This time Longarm couldn't restrain his laughter. He threw back his head and hooted, and Coffin, along with everybody else in the saloon, stared at him as if he had just lost his mind. Maybe he had, he thought wryly.

"What the hell's so funny?" Coffin demanded after a moment of listening to Longarm laugh.

"If you arrest me, old son, I reckon I'm going to have to arrest you. It's a federal crime to attack one of Uncle Sam's boys."

"You're a lawman too?" asked Coffin with a furious glare. "A federal man?"

"U.S. deputy marshal," Longarm confirmed. "And I'm

here in Del Rio on official business too, so I reckon I could charge you with interfering with my duties.''

''A U.S. marshal,'' repeated Coffin, his voice thick with both astonishment and anger. ''In Del Rio on official business.''

''That's right.''

''You're the fella they sent down from Denver.''

''Right again,'' Longarm told him.

Coffin groaned. ''My major's got me assigned to the same job that brought you here, Long. That means—''

Longarm nodded and said, ''Now you know why I was laughing. Looks like you and me are going to be working together, Coffin.''

Chapter 2

"You remember Don Alfredo Guiterrez, don't you, Custis?" Billy Vail had asked several days earlier in his office in the Denver Federal Building.

Longarm leaned back in the chair in front of the chief marshal's desk and used an iron-hard thumbnail to flick the head of a lucifer into flaming life. He held the match to the tip of the cheroot in his mouth and puffed until the tobacco was burning evenly. Then he shook out the lucifer, and dropped what was left of it on the floor next to the chair. That drew a frown from Vail. Longarm took the cheroot out of his mouth and shook his head. "Can't say as I do," he said.

"Well, you *do* recall that little dustup down in Arizona Territory last year, don't you?" Vail asked sarcastically. "In a little place called Inferno?"

Longarm frowned. He remembered Inferno, all right. It was there he had stumbled onto a madman's plan to kidnap the Vice President of the United States and a Mexican diplomat when those two important gents met in the little town for some secret negotiations concerning the border between their respective countries. Longarm had busted up that scheme and nearly got himself killed in the process, not to mention finding himself on the wrong side of a jail cell's bars a time or two during the whole mess. But that was long since over and done with.

"What's this fella Guiterrez got to do with what happened in Inferno?" asked Longarm.

"He was the representative from the Mexican government who was meeting with Vice President Wheeler."

Longarm shook his head. "Don't reckon I ever met him, or even heard his name. All I knew was that the Mexican government was sending somebody up there for the talks."

"Well, those talks are still going on, but now they're being moved to Del Rio, Texas, so that our government and the Mexicans can clear up any problems that might arise the next time the Rio Grande takes it into its head to change course." Vail cleared his throat. "This is confidential information, Custis, so don't go blabbing it all over the Palace Saloon."

Longarm shifted the cheroot from one corner of his mouth to the other. "Hell, Billy, you ought to know by now that I can keep a secret. I never said nothing to nobody about what happened in Inferno, except what was in my report to you."

"That's good, because we wanted to keep it quiet." Vail gave an exasperated sigh. "We even tried to see to it that the Mexican government didn't get wind of what almost happened, but they found out about it anyway. Guiterrez was in charge of the Mexican delegation, and he insisted on being told who was responsible for stopping that lunatic Vickery."

"So he found out my name," said Longarm with a shrug. "What's that got to do with me now?"

Vail rubbed a hand over his balding pink scalp. "Like I said, the negotiations have been moved to Del Rio, where they're scheduled to begin next Monday. Don Alfredo is still in charge of the Mexican delegation."

"Is the Vice President going down there?" asked Longarm.

Vail shook his head and said, "No, thank goodness. Politics has got him busy in Washington City, so he's turned everything over to the fella who was his assistant in the Inferno talks, a gent from the State Department named Franklin

Barton. Barton will be ramrodding our side this time around."

"All this politics and diplomacy ain't ever interested me overmuch, Billy," commented Longarm. "What's it got to do with me?"

"Since you pulled everybody's fat out of the fire down in Arizona, Guiterrez has requested that you be assigned to these negotiations as well, just to see that nothing goes wrong."

Longarm already had a pretty good idea that was going to be the answer. He suppressed a groan of dismay. "You mean I've got to go down to that Texas border country, which is going to be hotter'n the hinges of Hell at this time of year, and ride herd on a bunch of diplomats in swallowtail coats?"

Vail couldn't hold back a grin. "That seems to be about the size of it, all right, Custis."

Almost biting the cheroot in half, Longarm uttered a heartfelt "Shit."

"It won't be too bad," Vail assured him. "Everything's being kept even quieter than the first time, so there shouldn't be any trouble. I've already been in touch with Ranger headquarters in Austin, and Major Jones has promised to send a man down to Del Rio to give you a hand if you need it."

Longarm frowned. He had worked with the Texas Rangers before, sometimes amicably, sometimes not. The best of the so-called Frontier Battalion—Jim Hatfield, Sam Cody, Reese Bennett, men such as that—were top-notch lawmen, and Longarm could respect them even if they occasionally didn't have the same goals as he did. But there were other Rangers who were nothing but trouble.

"Jones say who he was sending?"

"Nope," replied Vail, "but I'm sure you'll get along just fine. There's not a better law enforcement agency west of the Mississippi than the Rangers. I used to ride with them, you know."

Longarm didn't need the reminder. He had heard Vail going on about how wonderful the Rangers were on more occasions than he liked to remember. "You sure there ain't some other job you need me on more?" he asked.

"I told you," Vail said sharply, "Don Alfredo asked for you in particular. We're eager to oblige in any little way we can, because we aim to ask the Diaz government for some concessions regarding the border."

Longarm held up a hand, palm out. "I don't need to hear about that part of it. I'll do my best to keep those old boys safe and sound, but whatever political business they hash out is their affair, not mine."

"Reckon that's a pretty good way to look it," Vail agreed. He glanced at the banjo clock on the wall. "Henry's got your orders and travel vouchers all waiting for you. Your train leaves in half an hour."

"Half an hour? Damn it, Billy—"

"That'll give you plenty of time to get your gear together, and we both know it," Vail said crisply. "So don't waste time arguing, Custis. I'll see you when you get back from Texas."

Not if I see you first, Longarm thought with ill grace.

But he had the sense to keep the comment to himself.

The Denver & Rio Grande took him as far as El Paso, following the river that gave the railroad part of its name down through New Mexico Territory. A while back, he had almost gotten thrown off a D&RG train by a would-be killer as the train was crossing a high trestle in New Mexico, so he stayed off the observation platforms on this trip. Besides, the mood he was in, it was easier just to stay in his seat and sulk. He hated bodyguarding politicians worse than almost anything. Not only was the job sometimes dangerous, but he had to listen to a lot more political bullshit than he liked.

From El Paso, he boarded a stagecoach that took him across West Texas, through country that was spectacularly beautiful in some places and spectacularly ugly in others. After a couple of days, the coach reached Del Rio, not far from where Devil's River flowed into the Rio Grande. It was a good-sized border town, with the surrounding countryside divided between cattle ranches and farms. A whole company of Texas Rangers had been stationed here at one time several years earlier, Longarm recalled when he arrived late on Sunday afternoon, but the post had been moved elsewhere as the area around Del Rio had settled down somewhat.

The first thing Longarm did was sign in at the hotel and stash his saddle, saddlebags, and Winchester in his room. He probably wouldn't need to rent a horse and do any riding on this job, but if he did, he would be ready. Then he headed for the sheriff's office to let the local lawman know that he was in town. According to Billy Vail, the sheriff, a man named Sanderson, knew something about the meeting that was going to take place in his town and had been sworn to secrecy.

Sanderson turned out to be not a very impressive-looking gent, in Longarm's opinion. The sheriff was below medium height, slope-shouldered, and could have used a shave. But his gaze was alert and intelligent as he looked across the desk in his office at the badge and bona fides Longarm was showing him.

"U.S. deppity marshal, huh?" Sanderson nodded. "I got a wire from your boss sayin' that you were on your way." He stood up and extended a hand across the desk. "Pleased to meet you, Marshal."

Longarm shook with him and found Sanderson's grip stronger than he figured it would be. The sheriff waved him into a ladder-back chair in front of the desk and went on. "What can I do for you?"

"Nothing in particular," said Longarm. "I just wanted to let you know that I was around."

"Well, that's mighty kind of you. I ain't been told exactly what's goin' to be happenin' around here for the next few days, but I know it's a mighty important meeting and that you're goin' to be keepin' an eye on things."

Longarm nodded. "That's right. There's supposed to be a Ranger coming in to give me a hand too. You know if he's in town yet?"

"Couldn't tell you," replied Sanderson with a shake of his head.

"You heard who it's going to be?"

"Nope. I'm just glad the gov'ment's sendin' both of you

down here right now, 'cause I got a full plate without havin' to worry about anything else."

"That so?" asked Longarm with a slight frown. "Been some trouble around here?"

"Aw, just a gang of owlhoots runnin' around and makin' life miserable for folks on both sides of the border. You ever hear of El Aguila?"

The name was vaguely familiar to Longarm, but he shook his head anyway. "Can't say as I have."

"He's pretty well known in these parts as an outlaw. Always ran by hisself before, but now I hear he's got a gang together, and they're the ones responsible for raidin' some of the ranches on both sides of the Rio. So far I ain't had much luck runnin' 'em to ground. But I will. You can count on that."

Longarm wasn't so sure, but it wasn't really any of his business. As long as this El Aguila and his gang steered clear of Del Rio while the negotiations were going on, that was all Longarm cared about.

He slipped his watch from his pocket and flipped it open to check the time. The heavy gold chain from the watch looped across the front of his vest from one pocket to the other, and at the other end of the chain was the little Colt derringer that had saved Longarm's life on more than one occasion. He put the watch away and said, "Nearly supper time. There a good place to eat around here?"

"Right across the street at the Red Top Cafe," said Sanderson with a grin. "Best steaks and fried chicken you'll find between here and San Antonio. And if you're of a mind for a drink later, Kilroy's Saloon just down the street'll fix you up just fine."

Longarm nodded as he stood up. "Much obliged. If that Ranger shows up, tell him I'm staying at the hotel, would you?"

"Sure."

"They have any Maryland rye down at Kilroy's?"

"They've got just about any kind of panther piss you're lookin' for, Marshal," Sanderson assured him.

Longarm grinned. "Then tell the Ranger he might be able

to find me there after a while, if I'm not at the hotel."

"You betcha." Sanderson waved a hand casually as Longarm walked out of the office.

Longarm ate supper at the Red Top, and while he was mulling over his steak he also mulled over everything Sanderson had told him. The idea that some outlaw gang was marauding in the area was vaguely disturbing, but it was unlikely they would come anywhere near Del Rio while the meetings were going on. Anyway, though the diplomats might not like it, Longarm intended to keep them cooped up in the hotel all the time they were there. That way they would be safe no matter what else was going on.

At least, he thought wryly, that was the plan.

After he ate, he strolled down the street and found Kilroy's Saloon. It took up almost a whole block, and its bat-winged entrance was on the corner of the building, so that a man could stand in front of the door and look down the boardwalk on two sides of the building. Music and laughter came from inside, and Longarm felt himself drawn by more than thirst. He went inside.

And found himself almost immediately being flirted with by the pretty redhead called Anna Marie. She was brazen about what she wanted, and Longarm had figured that she would wind up leading him upstairs.

Instead, he had been led right into a mess of trouble.

Lazarus Coffin glowered across the table at Longarm. "You *sure* you're a lawman?" demanded the Ranger.

"You saw my bona fides," Longarm reminded him, "just like I saw that badge of yours."

"You don't look like no federal man I ever saw."

Longarm started to return the veiled insult in kind, then stopped, because Coffin *did* look like a Texas Ranger—or at least he looked as much like one as anybody else, because the Rangers didn't have uniforms. What they had was a silver star in a silver circle, and that said it all.

Longarm sipped from the glass of rye that a bartender had brought over to the table, along with a bucket of beer for Coffin. "Folks around here seem to know you," said Longarm. "How'd that come to be, if you've just been sent down here from Austin?"

"Hell, I was raised in these parts," said Coffin. "And raised some hell o' my own too, if you know what I mean. Ain't many folks around here who don't know me."

An unsettling suspicion struck Longarm. "Just how long have you been a Ranger, Coffin?"

"Nigh on to six months now. Sheriff Sanderson suggested I might want to join up with 'em. There was this little, uh, misunderstandin' over some cattle that disappeared from a rancho on the other side o' the border."

Longarm closed his eyes and tried not to groan. He had been stuck with somebody who was not only a novice Ranger, but also probably a former rustler to boot. What the hell had Major John B. Jones been thinking when he sent Coffin down here to Del Rio on such a delicate assignment?

"All right," Longarm said with a sigh as he opened his eyes again. "We'd better get a few things straight between us. This is a federal matter, so you're just here to give me a hand. I'll be in charge of the arrangements."

Coffin's bearded jaw tightened, and he looked as if he wanted to argue the point. But after a moment, he nodded curtly. "That's what the major said. I reckon I'll follow orders—long as they ain't stupid."

"You'll follow orders," Longarm said flatly.

Coffin's brawny shoulders rose and fell in a shrug, and Longarm figured that was as close as he was going to get to an agreement. He moved on. "We both keep our mouths shut about what we're doing. There's been too much talk already. I'd rather we hadn't both stood there in the middle of the room and announced that we came here on an assignment, but I was a mite addled after that tussle with you."

Coffin took hold of his chin, moved his jaw back and forth, and winced. "You pack a pretty good punch, all right, Long. I wasn't thinkin' neither. Sorry."

Longarm drained the rest of his drink. "It shouldn't matter. I'm not expecting any trouble. We'll ride herd on those fellas from Washington and Mexico City for a few days, then they'll go home and so will we."

"What about El Aguila? I've heard tell his bunch is raidin' again."

Longarm shook his head. "This meeting shouldn't interest an owlhoot like El Aguila." He didn't mention it, but the man who had tried to kidnap the diplomats in Arizona had been an ex-military officer with a grudge against the government. That was a far cry from some minor border bandit, whose sights would likely be set a lot lower.

Still, Longarm couldn't ignore the possibility of trouble, so he continued. "Since you grew up around here, what do you know about El Aguila? That means The Eagle, doesn't it?"

"Yep," said Coffin with a nod. "I never saw the man. Nobody really knows who he is, 'cept maybe some of the Mexes along the river. They claim to know, but they're mighty closemouthed whenever the subject comes up. El Aguila's got a reputation for hornin' in on schemes that other folks come up with, but he ain't never run with a gang of his own until now."

"You're sure he's ramrodding this bunch?"

"That's what the reports the major's gotten say. I figure when this business here in Del Rio's over, I might take a few days 'fore I head back to Austin and try to help Sheriff Sanderson catch the skunk."

"More power to you," said Longarm. "Just make sure this job is over and done with first."

"Sure, sure," Coffin said with a wave of his hand. He slurped down some of the beer, then surprised Longarm by saying, "No hard feelin's 'bout that fracas earlier, right?"

"No hard feelings," Longarm agreed. "We've got to work together, so we might as well try to get along."

"Yeah." Coffin looked sheepishly down at the table. "I didn't really mean all those things I said to Anna Marie. I think she's really mighty sweet, and she sure is pretty. It's just that . . . well, when you're a big ol' galoot like I am, folks sort of expect you to bull around and raise a ruckus. You savvy?"

Longarm shrugged. "Whatever you say, Coffin. That ain't really any of my business neither."

The big Ranger grinned. "Like I said, you pack a wallop. You reckon Anna Marie's still mad at me?"

"I wouldn't be surprised," Longarm said.

Coffin put his hands on the table and pushed himself to his feet. "I'm goin' up to her room and find out. See you, Long."

"Be at the hotel first thing in the morning," Longarm reminded him.

Coffin nodded his head to show he had heard, but didn't look back. Longarm chuckled tiredly. Coffin had his mind set on Anna Marie again, but Longarm figured he would be lucky if the redhead didn't bust something over his skull when he came knocking on her door. She had a temper to match her hair.

Longarm stood up and headed for the door of the saloon. He intended to go back to the hotel. It had been a long day, and he was tired. And as soon as those diplomats arrived in the morning, he was going to be responsible for their safety, so he wanted a good night's sleep.

Even though he was confident there wasn't going to be any trouble, it never hurt to be careful. . . .

Chapter 3

As soon as he reached the door of his hotel room, Longarm knew that a good night's sleep was going to be postponed, at least for a while. The second-floor corridor was lit by lamps that hung at each end of the hallway, and while the light wasn't particularly good, it was bright enough for Longarm to see that the match he'd wedged low down between the door and the jamb was no longer there. Instead, he saw the end of it peeking out from underneath the door, where it had fallen unnoticed when somebody had opened the door.

An uninvited guest had been in the room—or maybe was still there.

Longarm's hand went to the butt of his gun. He had hesitated for only a second when he noticed that the telltale match had been disturbed, and he hoped that that pause hadn't been detected by the person who was waiting inside the room, if indeed the intruder was still present. Longarm drew the gun as he used his left hand to slide the key into the lock and turn it. He didn't try to be quiet about it. Stealth would just give away his suspicions. Instead he threw the door open suddenly and went diving through it, rolling and coming up in a crouch with the Colt leveled and his finger on the trigger.

Anna Marie gasped, drew back against the headboard of the bed, and pulled the sheet higher around her. But not so high, noted Longarm, that the big brown nipple of her left breast was covered up.

"What in blazes are you doing here?" Longarm asked harshly.

The redhead conquered the fear that had gripped her at Longarm's abrupt entry into the hotel room. "What do you think, Custis?" she asked. "I came to see you."

"That fella Coffin is looking for you," said Longarm as he holstered his gun. "I just left him over at Kilroy's, heading up to your room."

Anna Marie made a face. "Then he will be disappointed, won't he?"

Longarm's eyes strayed back to that insistent nipple as he said, "Seemed to me like maybe the two of you were . . . involved."

She shook her head emphatically. "No. I have known Lazarus for a long time, and he has always been in love with me. But the feeling is one I do not return."

"He's got a funny way of showing it. He was downright mean to you."

She shrugged, and the sheet she clutched in her hands slipped enough so that the nipple of her right breast peeked out too. "That has always been his way. He treats me badly, then he is sorry and tries to make up for it. Tonight, though, when he grabbed my wrist, was the first time he has actually hurt me. Always before he just said cruel things." She looked down, no longer meeting Longarm's gaze. "I know what I am. He does not have to call me those ugly names."

"I'm sorry," Longarm said. He took his hat off and tossed it on the mirrored dresser on one side of the room.

Anna Marie slid toward him, letting the sheet fall even farther. "You will not make me go back over there, will you, Custis? I would much rather be with you."

Longarm stepped over to the bed and reached down to cup her left breast. His thumb toyed with the erect nipple as he said, "I ain't in the habit of kicking pretty women out of my bed unless they're married or plan on killing me."

She smiled up at him and leaned toward him a little so that more of her ample breast filled his hand. "I am not married, as you know, and as for killing you . . . only the little death will we share tonight."

Longarm had shared more than a few of those "little deaths" with a variety of willing women. He smiled as he reached for Anna Marie's other breast. As he caressed the creamy globes, she threw her head back and closed her eyes, obviously enjoying the way he kneaded the soft flesh and strummed the pebbled nipples with his thumbs.

With her eyes still closed, she reached out and clasped his thighs through his trousers. Her hands ran up his legs to his crotch, and she began to deftly unfasten the buttons of his fly with one hand while she used the other to trace the length and heft of his shaft, which was already hard and throbbing.

Longarm's fingers squeezed harder on her breasts as Anna Marie delved inside his pants and freed his manhood. It jutted out from his groin, proudly erect. She closed both hands around it, and the heat of her grip made his hips surge forward a little. She tipped her head forward again and opened her eyes, staring in amazement at the pole of stiff flesh she was holding.

"Custis, you are a lot of man!" she exclaimed. She leaned forward, examining his maleness at closer range. Her tongue stole from her mouth to lick across her lips, and Longarm bit back a groan. She gave him a mischievous grin, then opened her lips wide and took him into her mouth.

Longarm put his hands on her shoulders to balance himself as she sucked him in, her lips closing tightly around the shaft. Her tongue circled the head in warm, wet swipes that made a shudder go through him. She slid over to the edge of the bed so that she wouldn't have to stretch so far to reach him, and that enabled her to swallow even more of him. She reached around him with her right arm, her fingers grabbing hold of his butt to steady him, while her left hand dropped between her widespread legs. She grunted and sucked harder as she began to play with herself.

He couldn't stand much of this, Longarm knew. And satisfying as it no doubt would have been, he didn't want to spend his climax in her mouth. When he felt it approaching, he gently pushed her back and slid his shaft out of her mouth. She made a little sound of disappointment.

That quickly turned to a squeal of delight as Longarm laid her down on the bed and put his hands on the insides of her thighs, spreading them even wider. The feminine folds were completely open to him now, and he saw drops of dew sparkling in the thick bush of red hair that covered her mound. He put his thumbs on each side of the slit and peeled the folds back even more as he bent his head between her thighs. His tongue speared into her, making her gasp and clutch at his head, tangling her fingers in his hair.

Her legs, bent far back at the knees, sawed back and forth, her thighs closing and opening against his ears, as he licked and sucked on her core. The opening was drenched, and searing heat rose from it as he explored it with his tongue. She cried out, scissoring her legs around his head once more, then pleaded, "Oh, Custis, now, please now!"

Longarm's face was smeared with her juices as he lifted his head and began discarding his clothes haphazardly. In a matter of seconds, he was as naked as she was and moving over her. She reached down for his shaft and brought it to her opening, and with a powerful surge of his hips, he thrust into her. She gave a muffled scream, then reached up and twined her arms around his neck, pulling his face down to hers. Their open mouths came together and her tongue dueled frantically with his. She had to be tasting her own juices, he thought as she licked frenziedly at his tongue and the inside of his mouth. He pumped into her, driving hard and fast.

Neither of them expected this part to last very long, and it didn't. When Longarm felt his climax boiling up this time, he didn't try to stop it. He just drove himself to the deepest point yet and held his shaft there as it began to spew his seed in throbbing spurts. He emptied everything of himself into her, filling her completely, and she was carried over the crest with him, bucking and surging beneath him as her head thrashed back and forth. He lifted himself on his hands and watched her through slitted eyes as he poured his climax into her. The telltale flush of her own culmination spread across her chest above the bobbing breasts.

Exhaustion washed over him in an inexorable tide. Barely able to keep himself from collapsing on top of her, he rolled to the side and sprawled on the bed next to her. For a few moments, he had forgotten how hot the nights could be here along the Rio Grande, but now he realized that he was covered with sweat and so was Anna Marie. As he tried to catch his breath, he said, "Wonder if we could . . . get a tub of water up here . . . so we could take a bath."

"I think perhaps it could be arranged," she said as she snuggled against his side and slid the palm of her hand over his chest and the flat stomach beneath it to the thicket of dark hair around his now-soft manhood. She leaned her head closer to him and her teeth nipped playfully at his ear. "I think we could even find a tub large enough for both of us to bathe at the same time."

"Sounds like a good idea to me," said Longarm. He grinned. "Saves water that way."

Only, what with one thing and another, they splashed out a considerable amount of the water that was carried up in buckets by Mexican servants and dumped in the big tin tub the night clerk brought up. And Longarm wound up not getting to sleep until well after midnight.

But when he finally dozed off, he was scrubbed clean—and so sated that he figured he might not ever want to make love again.

Thankfully, by morning he was over that feeling. In fact, he woke up wishing that Anna Marie was still beside him. But she had slipped out sometime far into the night to return to her own room at Kilroy's.

Just as well, Longarm told himself grumpily as he dragged out of bed and splashed clean water on his face from the basin on the dresser. He had work to do this morning.

The orders he had been given in Denver by Henry, Billy Vail's clerk, stated that the American delegation headed by Franklin Barton would arrive this morning on a special stagecoach. Likewise, the coach carrying Don Alfredo Guiterrez and the other members of the Mexican delegation was supposed to be pulling into Ciudad Acuna, Del Rio's sister city across the Rio Grande, by midday. Longarm felt fairly confident that Barton and the other diplomats from Washington would show up on schedule. He was less sure that the Mexicans would be on time. Mexico City was closer to the border than Washington, but the country in between was a lot rougher and had more potential for delays. Both groups knew they were supposed to meet at this hotel, so Longarm figured to stick fairly close unless circumstances warranted otherwise.

He shaved, put on a clean shirt, and went downstairs to have breakfast in the hotel dining room. The smell of coffee made him perk up, as did the sight of a buxom blond waitress in a starched apron. She hurried up to the table he had chosen and gave him a friendly smile as he sat down.

"Coffee?" she asked.

"Black and hot and plenty of it," said Longarm. He glanced at a menu chalked on a blackboard on the wall behind the counter and went on. "Bring me a stack of flapjacks, a pile of fried potatoes, and as much bacon as you can fit onto the plate around 'em. Better have a steak and some gravy on the side too."

"Goodness, you must be hungry this morning." The woman's smile widened. "What did you do last night to work up such an appetite, sir?"

Longarm patted his belly and returned her grin. "I'm just a growing boy," he said, though he hadn't been a boy of any kind since he'd left the mountains of West-by-God Virginia all those years ago, during the Late Unpleasantness.

The waitress laughed and hurried off to begin filling his order. Longarm glanced around the dining room. It was early, with sunrise still a quarter hour away, but quite a few customers were seated at the tables scattered around the room. More men were sitting at the counter. Most of the diners were townsmen who probably stopped here for breakfast every day before going on to their businesses. Longarm saw a few cowboys, all of whom seemed to have hangovers. The lawman chuckled as he noted the greenish tinge on their faces. He remembered all too well what it was like to be young and sick as a dog from too much Who-hit-John the night before.

He had been sitting there only a few minutes when a big figure loomed in the arched entrance that led to the hotel lobby. Lazarus Coffin had a scowl on his face, and the townsmen who glanced at him looked away quickly, unwilling to meet his squinty-eyed glare. Coffin spotted Longarm and started across the room toward the table, moving stiffly as if his muscles were sore. Longarm knew *that* feeling quite well too. He had some aches and pains this morning from the ruckus with Coffin the night before.

"You seen Anna Marie?" Coffin demanded as he came up to the table. "I never did find her last night so's I could tell her how sorry I am."

"Haven't seen hide nor hair of her this morning," Longarm replied truthfully. He hoped Coffin wouldn't press the issue. The last thing he wanted was another brawl with the massive Texas Ranger. With a wave at the chair on the other side of the table, Longarm said, "Have a seat and join me for breakfast."

"Don't mind if I do," said Coffin. "I'm so damn hungry my belly thinks my throat's been cut." As he sat down, he turned his head in the general direction of the counter and bellowed, "Coffee, damn it!"

Longarm saw the cowboys wince as Coffin's roar assaulted their fragile senses. Coffin looked a little green around the gills himself, but if he was feeling the effects of too much whiskey the night before, he seemed determined not to let it bother him. Longarm asked, "You got any thoughts on how we ought to go about the job that brought us both here?"

"You mean—" Coffin began loudly, then stopped, remembering that Longarm didn't want a lot of talk about the specifics of their mission. Lowering his voice, he continued. "I figured we'd just corral them old boys here in the hotel."

Longarm nodded. "That was my thought too. They ain't coming here to sightsee, so they might as well stay inside and get their work done."

The blond waitress approached the table tentatively carrying a tray that contained a pot of coffee and two cups. She set it on the table and then scurried back a couple of steps, as if afraid that Coffin would lash out at her. The Ranger didn't seem to notice how badly he'd spooked her.

"Damn well about time," muttered Coffin as he filled one of the cups and then passed the coffeepot to Longarm. Longarm took it carefully, using the piece of leather that was wrapped around the handle to keep from burning his fingers. While Longarm was filling his own cup, Coffin slurped down about half of the blistering hot brew, then smacked his lips. "Not quite strong enough, but I reckon it'll do."

Any stronger and it would have eaten a hole in the cup, Longarm thought as he sipped the stuff.

Sheriff Sanderson strolled into the dining room, spotted his fellow lawmen, and came across the room to join them. He was wearing a battered old hat and a stained vest this morning. "Hidy," he greeted Longarm and Coffin. "Mind if I sit down?"

"Help yourself," said Longarm with a gesture at one of the two remaining empty chairs. Sanderson sat down and dropped his hat on the floor beside him. His thinning brown hair looked as if it hadn't seen a comb in weeks.

Sanderson and Coffin made quite a pair, Longarm thought as he looked at them. They were about as disreputable-looking as any badge-toters he had ever run across. But how they looked wasn't nearly as important as how well they did their jobs, and so far Longarm didn't have any real evidence either way on that score.

The sheriff motioned for the waitress to bring him a coffee cup. When she had done that, Sanderson picked up the pot and looked over at Coffin. "You been behavin' yourself since you went up to Austin and joined the Rangers, Lazarus?"

"Sure I have," said Coffin. "I been a model citizen, Sheriff."

Sanderson grunted. "You best stay that way, or you'll wind up in my jail again. Couldn't hardly believe it last night when somebody told me you was the Ranger sent down here to give Marshal Long a hand."

Coffin's bearded jaw tightened. "No offense to Long here, but they didn't need to send no federal lawman. I coulda taken care o' things just fine by my ownself."

"It never hurts to have two good men on a job," Longarm said mildly.

"It might if they keep trippin' over one another," said Coffin.

"That won't happen." Longarm's voice was flat, but it left no room for argument.

The three men kept the waitress busy for the next half hour as she hurried back and forth between the table and the kitchen, carrying platters of food that seemed to be consumed almost before she could make it back to the kitchen. As Longarm would have expected, Coffin was a prodigious eater, and the sheriff put away quite a bit of food for a medium-sized fella. Longarm's own appetite was keen this morning, and he wasn't satisfied until he had cleaned four plates of his own.

Finally, Coffin leaned back in his chair and patted his stomach. "Reckon I've exercised the ol' table muscle enough." He let out a loud belch and undid the top button of his denim pants.

"You're still a crude son of a bitch, ain't you, Lazarus?" said Sanderson. Coffin just grinned at him. Sanderson put a little more coffee in his cup and turned to Longarm. "Anything special you want me to do whilst you're in town, Marshal?"

"Nope," said Longarm. "Until we see how things are going to go, we won't know exactly what we'll need to be doing." He checked his watch. "It'll still be a while before the parties from both sides get here."

Sanderson's chair scraped as he pushed it back and stood up. "Well, I reckon I'd better mosey on then. I'll make my mornin' rounds, make sure nothin' happened durin' the night."

The sheriff fished some coins out of his pocket and left them on the table to pay for his breakfast, then started slowly toward the door. Longarm had the feeling that the local lawman didn't get in any hurry unless he had to. A glance out the front window of the dining room showed Longarm that the sun was up now, the reddish-gold slanting rays lighting the street outside.

Illuminating, as well, were the armed men who suddenly raced by on horseback, yelling and shooting.

Chapter 4

For an instant, Longarm sat there, too stunned by the sudden outbreak of violence to move. Then instincts honed by long years in a very dangerous profession took hold, and he surged up out of his chair, overturning it behind him. His hand flashed to his gun and jerked the Colt from its holster.

"What the hell!" shouted Sheriff Sanderson. Hard on the heels of his startled exclamation, the front window of the dining room shattered in a million pieces, sending a spray of glass across the room. Longarm threw up his left arm to protect his eyes from the flying slivers. He knew that one of the bullets being tossed around so recklessly by the men outside had struck the window.

A glance told Longarm that Lazarus Coffin was on his feet too. The pearl-handled Remington was in the big Ranger's hand. Sanderson had drawn his gun as well. All three men lunged for the entrance to the lobby, leaving the screams and shouts and chaos of the dining room behind them. Sanderson was closer, but Longarm and Coffin had longer legs. They reached the lobby at about the same time and raced across it, bursting out onto the boardwalk in front of the hotel.

"El Aguila! El Aguila!"

The terrified shout came from down the street somewhere.

At least a dozen masked men were galloping through Del Rio, strung out in a long line. Some of them were still passing the hotel. The sound of gunfire and the stench of burned powder filled the air as the raiders emptied their weapons in a careless orgy of death. Longarm saw several luckless victims already sprawled on the planks further along the boardwalk.

He went to one knee and lifted the Colt, triggering it as one of the riders flashed past him. The weapon bucked against his palm, and Longarm had the satisfaction of seeing the masked owlhoot jerk sideways in the saddle. The man didn't fall, but he clutched desperately at his saddlehorn and sagged forward, clearly hit hard by Longarm's bullet.

Close beside him he heard the roar of Coffin's Remington and the whiplash of Sanderson's smaller-caliber revolver. Another of the outlaws was hit, and this one tumbled off his mount to slam into the ground in a tangle of arms and legs like a child's carelessly discarded rag doll. "Got him!" Sheriff Sanderson crowed, and immediately Coffin protested, "The hell you did! That was my bullet took the bastard down!"

Longarm came to his feet. The last of the raiders had galloped past, but they were turning around at the far end of the street. "No need to argue, boys," said Longarm dryly. "Looks like there'll be plenty of those desperadoes to go around—*'cause here they come again!*"

Sure enough, the marauders were launching a second attack on the town. This time Longarm got a look at the man in the lead. Not much of his face was visible between a pulled-up bandanna and a tugged-down Stetson, but Longarm could tell he was a big, broad-shouldered man, built along lines similar to Lazarus Coffin, but not as massive. Longarm snapped a shot at the leader, but figured it missed, since the man showed no sign of being hit as he led the charge once more past the hotel. This time, Longarm, Coffin, and Sanderson had to throw themselves flat on the boardwalk as the outlaws returned their fire. Slugs thudded into the wall and chewed splinters from the railing along the edge of the boardwalk. As a bullet smacked into one of the planks only a few inches from Longarm's head, he knew he had to hunt some cover.

He rolled quickly toward the edge of the boardwalk and dropped the foot and a half to the ground. That put him between the boardwalk and one of the watering troughs that lined the street. The ground was a little muddy there, since horses had obviously been drinking earlier and had dripped quite a bit from their muzzles, but Longarm didn't worry about getting a little mud on his clothes. The thick wood of the trough and the water inside it would stop the outlaw lead from reaching him.

Longarm glanced behind him and saw that Coffin and Sanderson had overturned the heavy wooden bench that normally sat on the far side of the hotel doors. Most days, that bench was occupied by hotel visitors and various old-timers passing the time. Now it was serving as a shield behind which the sheriff and the Ranger crouched as they shot it out with the raiders. Sanderson had no trouble getting his slight frame behind the overturned bench, but Coffin was so big that he stuck out in places.

Longarm had three shots left in his Colt, and he emptied them as fast as he could pull the trigger as he raised up behind the water trough. One of the outlaws' horses stumbled but didn't go down. Then, as quickly as it had happened before, the riders were past the hotel. Scattered gunfire came from elsewhere along the street as a few of Del Rio's citizens tried to put up a fight. At this hour of the morning, though, folks were still sleepy, and certainly weren't prepared to fight for their lives against a gang of vicious killers.

And the outlaws were already regrouping at the end of the street for yet another sweep through the town.

Longarm jammed his Colt back in its holster as he pushed himself to his feet and bounded up onto the boardwalk. He headed for the door of the hotel, ignoring Coffin's angry shout, "Where you goin', Long?" It probably looked to Coffin and Sanderson as if he was running out on this fight, but Longarm figured he could do more damage if he could get his hands on the Winchester up in his room.

He charged across the lobby, barely noticing the clerk peeking fearfully over the counter from where he crouched behind it. Longarm didn't see any of the guests, and hoped they all had the sense to lie low. He took the stairs three at a time, then dashed down the second-floor corridor when he reached the landing. He had rigged the door of his room with a match again when he left earlier, but now there was no time to check it before he flung the door open. No one was waiting to ambush him. He snatched up the Winchester, which he had left leaning in a corner, and dug a box of cartridges out of his saddlebags. Fumbling out a handful of the .44-40s, he began thumbing them into the rifle's loading gate as he hurried across the hall to a room that was on the front of the hotel.

Longarm lifted a booted foot and slammed it against the door of the other room, not taking the time to worry about whether or not it was occupied. As luck had it, it wasn't. He sprang to the window, hearing the pounding of hoofbeats from the street, followed by the bang of more gunshots.

Longarm shoved the window up and leaned out as he jacked a shell into the chamber of the Winchester. The outlaws were just reaching the hotel again. From somewhere below him, pistols cracked as Coffin and Sanderson opened fire on them. Longarm jerked the rifle to his shoulder and drew a quick bead on one of the riders. When he squeezed off the shot, the outlaw went flying out of the saddle like a pinwheel.

As fast as he could work the rifle's lever, Longarm raked El Aguila's gang with deadly accurate fire. Two more men fell. Between them, the three lawmen had accounted for almost half of the outlaws, and when their murderous charge reached the end of the street this time, the surviving members of the gang kept going. They were headed south, toward the Rio Grande, and Longarm had little doubt that within minutes, they would be splashing across the border river into Mexico. There was no point in going after them.

But they had left four men on the street behind them, and Longarm was certain several more had been badly wounded. Carrying the Winchester, he hurried downstairs and found Coffin and Sanderson in the street, checking the bodies of the fallen outlaws.

"We got one dead and three that soon will be," said Sanderson as he looked up at Longarm. "Figured that was you when that rifle opened up. Good shootin', Marshal."

"What do you mean, good shootin'?" demanded Coffin with a snort. The Remington was still in his hand, and he waved at the dead and unconscious outlaws. "I was the one who downed these coyotes, all four of 'em!"

Longarm knew better than that, but he didn't think it was worth an argument. He walked into the street and looked at each of the bodies in turn. None of them belonged to the big man who had been leading the outlaws.

To the sheriff, Longarm said, "That big jigger, I reckon he was El Aguila?"

Sanderson shrugged. "Hell, your guess is as good as mine about that, Marshal. That fella looked like he was in charge of the raid, but maybe he just got stuck ridin' in front and couldn't do nothin' about it. Anyway, he ain't here, and it ain't likely any of these boys'd be willin' to talk even if they come to 'fore they die, which ain't likely neither."

Longarm had to admit that Sanderson was probably right. Even as he nodded grimly, he heard a death rattle from the throat of one of the wounded outlaws. A white-haired old man carrying a black medical bag was hurrying down the street, but he was going to be too late to do much good. Sanderson advised him of as much, calling out, "No need to hurry, Doc."

Both of the other outlaws died as the elderly physician was checking their wounds. The doctor shook his head and looked up at the three lawmen. "There was nothing I could do."

"Don't waste any sympathy on these rabid skunks, Doc," said Sanderson. He sighed. "I'd best go fetch the undertaker."

Sanderson had just taken a few steps down the street when a man wearing a nightshirt with a pair of trousers hastily pulled on over it came running up to him. "Sheriff!" the man cried. "They . . . they got into the bank!"

Sanderson caught hold of the man's arm to steady him. "What'd you say, Ames?"

Longarm figured the man for the town banker. He had the

well-fed look about him common to such men, and he certainly seemed distraught enough as he gasped out, "The back door of the bank . . . they broke it down! While the others rode up and down the street shooting . . . safe was looted . . . thousands of dollars gone . . . I thought I had better check, just in case. . . ."

What he was saying made sense, thought Longarm. While the rest of the gang had kept the whole town occupied, a few of the outlaws had managed to get into the bank and open the safe. Usually that took dynamite, but there were some slick-fingered gents who could tickle a combination lock until it opened. Obviously, El Aguila had one of those criminally talented individuals riding with him.

Sanderson was cussing up a storm as he stomped off with the banker. The news of the robbery had made him forget about going for the undertaker, but that didn't really matter. Longarm saw a man in a black suit driving a wagon down the street toward the hotel, and figured that he was the local planter. In this border heat, undertakers had to move fast. Even though the sun still wasn't high, it was already shining down with a brassy intensity.

Coffin let out a low whistle. "I'm almighty glad those fellas from Washington ain't already here."

"You and me both," agreed Longarm. "From the way the sheriff was talking about El Aguila's gang, I didn't think they'd hit the town. They've been just raiding the ranches hereabouts, on both sides of the border."

"Reckon they decided there was more *dinero* to be made in bank-robbin' than there is in rustlin'. They musta been readin' about Jesse James."

Longarm didn't know about that. All he could be sure of was that with El Aguila now targeting Del Rio too, the job that had brought him here might have just gotten a lot harder.

By mid-morning, most of the signs that a pitched battle had briefly been fought in the town's main street had been cleaned up. The dead townspeople and outlaws had been carted away by the undertaker, and the blood they had spilled had been soaked up by the thirsty ground. The bullet holes in the buildings had been plastered over. The most noticeable damage was the missing window in the hotel dining room. It would take several days for a new pane of glass big enough to fill the window to be freighted over from San Antonio, so in the meantime the gaping hole had boards nailed over it. That would cut down on the light in the dining room, but it was better than letting in hordes of flies.

Longarm leaned on the boardwalk railing and looked out at the street. He was debating just how much to tell the diplomats about the dangers they might be facing from marauding outlaws. Heavy footsteps sounded on the planks behind him, and a big hand fell on his shoulder.

"What you frownin' about, Long?" asked Lazarus Coffin. "You ain't still worried 'bout them owlhoots, are you?"

"The thought that they might cause a little trouble *did* cross my mind."

"Naw," said Coffin, shaking his head. He tipped his broad-brimmed sombrero back. "We can handle El Aguila's bunch if we have to. Hell, we already did so much damage to 'em that they're probably still ridin' deeper into Mexico. Mark my words, they ain't comin' back here to Del Rio any time soon."

"I hope you're right," said Longarm. "But I reckon I'll believe it when I see it." His eyes narrowed as he gazed toward the northern end of the street. "Speaking of seeing things . . ."

A small cloud of dust was rising in the distance. It was just the right size, thought Longarm, to be kicked up by the hooves of a team pulling a stagecoach. The regular coach on the line that served Del Rio wasn't due for two more days; that was one of the things Longarm had checked. So it stood to reason that the vehicle rolling toward town now was the special coach carrying Franklin Barton and the other members of the American negotiating party.

Coffin had spotted the same dust cloud. "Reckon that must be them," he said. "You ready, Long?"

"Ready to be saddled with a bunch of politicians from back East?" Longarm chuckled grimly. "Not hardly. But we don't have much choice in the matter, do we?"

They watched the approach of the stagecoach for a few moments. Then abruptly, Coffin nudged Longarm with an elbow. "Look down yonder," he said, inclining his head toward the south.

Longarm looked, and he saw a similar cloud of dust coming from that direction. The Rio Grande was a couple of miles away from Del Rio, and judging by the dust that was rising to the south of town, another coach had already crossed the river and was rolling north.

"Now that's what you call timin'," said Coffin. "Looks like both bunches're goin' to get here at just about the same time."

Longarm looked back and forth, estimating the distances, and knew that Coffin was right. The coaches would arrive within minutes of each other. The one coming from the south had to be carrying Don Alfredo Guiterrez and the rest of the Mexican party.

Inexplicably, Longarm felt a tingle of apprehension. It prickled along his spine and made the hair on the back of his neck stand up for a second. He tried to blame it on the earlier violence and the fact that El Aguila's gang might indeed represent a threat to the meetings between the two governments. But all his instincts told him that wasn't the case.

This was something new, something that had come out of nowhere.

The American coach arrived first. Longarm wasn't sure whose idea it had been to send a special coach with the diplomats to Del Rio. If the idea was to not attract much attention, this was a piss-poor way of going about it. The arrival of the regularly scheduled stage was enough to provoke plenty of curiosity on the part of the townspeople; this unscheduled stop immediately drew quite a crowd. The coach was a standard Concord model with *Wells, Fargo & Co.* written in curling script above the door. No doubt the government had chartered it special for the trip, Longarm thought—and at a lot higher price than it was worth too.

The jehu and the shotgun guard were both roughly dressed, grizzled, and bearded, typical specimens of their profession. The driver brought the coach to an easy stop in front of the hotel. A man in a dark, sober suit that reminded Longarm of a preacher's outfit opened the door and stepped out first. Despite the civilian clothes, he had a crisp way of moving that cried out "Army" to Longarm. The fella practically saluted as he held the door open for the other men who began to disembark from the coach.

The second man off the stage paused on the ground to brush dust from his suit and bowler hat. He was on the young side of middle age, with dark sandy hair and a mustache. Pale blue eyes landed on Longarm, and the man stepped toward him. "Custis Long?" he asked. Longarm noted that the man didn't address him as a marshal.

"That's right," said Longarm. He stepped down from the boardwalk and extended his hand.

The man shook it, his grip firm. "Franklin Barton," he said, introducing himself. He turned to indicate the two men who had followed him off the stage. "This is Thaddeus Quine and Lewis Markson." Still no mention of anything to indicate who they really were.

Longarm nodded to Quine and Markson. Both of them were pasty-faced gents, one thin and one portly, and both looked thoroughly miserable to find themselves here on the frontier. They would have been much more comfortable in the offices and drawing rooms of Washington.

That left the military man, whom Franklin Barton introduced as Jeffery Spooner. Longarm figured Spooner for a lieutenant, maybe a captain. He would have been sent along to keep an eye on the diplomats during the journey down here to Del Rio, but now that they were here, Longarm expected to take over the main part of that chore. He hoped he wouldn't have any trouble from Spooner.

Barton clapped his hat back on his head and rubbed his hands together. "Well, I suppose you have rooms reserved for us here in the hotel," he said to Longarm.

"Yes, sir. Coffin and I will take your bags up."

"Hell," rumbled Coffin, "I ain't no porter."

Barton looked the Ranger up and down and seemed unimpressed, even a little dismayed, by what he saw. Longarm could understand the feeling. "And who might you be?" asked Barton.

"Lazarus Coffin, Texas Ranger. And I ain't takin' no sass from no fancy dude—"

"Coffin!" Longarm's voice lashed out. "I said you and me would get the bags. That's what we're going to do. Remember who's in charge here."

"I am," Franklin Barton said with more than a hint of arrogance in his voice, "but I know what you mean, Mr. Long. Come along, gentlemen." Without looking back to make sure that *somebody* was fetching the bags, Barton led his companions into the hotel.

Longarm and Coffin glowered at each other for a moment. Then with a disgusted sigh, Coffin headed for the canvas-covered boot at the rear of the coach. The diplomats' bags would be stored there.

Before the two lawmen could do anything else, the arrival of the second coach made them turn to greet it. Unlike the Wells, Fargo vehicle that had brought Barton and the other American diplomats to Del Rio, this coach was fancy, painted a high glossy black that gleamed even under the coating of dust that had settled on it during the trip. The horses pulling it were magnificent animals. Comparing them to a regular stage team was like comparing night and day. Clearly, Don Alfredo Guiterrez liked to travel in style.

A man in a flat-crowned hat, charro jacket, and ruffled shirt was the first one out of the coach. Longarm took him to be a servant, especially from the quick way he turned around and reached back up to help the next occupant of the coach step down. Longarm expected that to be Don Alfredo.

Instead, a woman's delicate foot emerged from the coach, followed by a trim ankle that showed momentarily underneath the swirling skirt of an elaborately tailored traveling outfit. Clasping the man's hand, the woman stepped down from the coach and looked around, her eyes bright and practically flashing with excitement.

"Son of a bitch," Coffin breathed as he stood beside Longarm, gaping at the woman. It wasn't a curse.

And Longarm knew exactly how he felt.

Chapter 5

Longarm realized he was staring, but at least he wasn't standing there with his mouth open like Coffin. He prodded the Ranger in the ribs with an elbow. "That gal's with one of those Mexican diplomats," Longarm hissed. "You want to cause a war by gawping at her like that?"

Coffin swallowed hard. "What I want is to—"

Longarm tromped on Coffin's foot to shut the Ranger up as he stepped forward and took off his hat. A man was disembarking from the coach behind the young woman, and his dark eyes were slitted suspiciously as he looked at Longarm.

"Welcome to Del Rio," said Longarm. "Are you Don Alfredo Guiterrez, señor?"

"I am," the man said crisply. He was tall and lean, clean-shaven, and had thick iron-gray hair under his flat-crowned hat.

"I'm Custis Long," Longarm went on as he extended his hand. "It's good to meet you, sir."

Don Alfredo's stiff attitude relaxed a little. He shook Longarm's hand and said, "Ah, the famous Custis Long. I understand you did me a great favor last year, Señor Long."

"Well, at the time I was just trying to stay alive, but I figure it worked out pretty well for you and Vice President

Wheeler too. You wouldn't have enjoyed the hospitality of that fella I ran into in Inferno."

Coffin said, "What the hell are you talkin' about? You didn't tell me none of this, Long."

"Ancient history," Longarm said with a wave of his hand. "Don Alfredo, this is Lazarus Coffin. He's lending a hand with things here on behalf of the State of Texas."

The diplomat's eyes narrowed again as he looked at Coffin. Most people seemed to have that reaction, thought Longarm.

"You are a Texas Ranger?" Guiterrez asked.

Coffin's broad chest puffed out. "That's right," he said defiantly.

The young woman stepped forward and put her hand on Don Alfredo's arm. "Papa, must we stand in the hot sun while you talk with these handsome men?"

"Of course not, dearest," said Guiterrez. He patted her hand, then looked at Longarm and Coffin again. "Gentlemen, this is my daughter Sonia. I expect you to see that she is well protected while I am here."

Coffin began, "Shoot, I'd be glad to—"

Longarm interrupted him again, moving in front of him and nodding politely to Sonia Guiterrez. "Very pleased to meet you, señorita. Your rooms are right here in the hotel. Mr. Coffin and I will see that your bags are unloaded and taken upstairs."

Sonia favored him with a smile, and Longarm felt it down to his toes. "*Muchas gracias*, Señor Long."

It wasn't that she was astoundingly beautiful, Longarm thought as he stepped back, forcing Coffin to do so as well, so that Don Alfredo and his daughter could step up onto the boardwalk and enter the hotel. Sonia's mouth was a little too wide and her nose was a bit too prominent. Longarm had known plenty of women who were prettier.

But seldom had he encountered a woman who possessed the indefinable *something* Sonia had. There was a certain air about her . . . an air that practically screamed that she would like nothing more than to be flat on her back with her legs wantonly flung wide as she welcomed a lucky man into her body.

She was of medium height and not skinny by any means. The lush curves of her body were revealed by the expensive traveling outfit. Her hair was a mass of curls that were a dark, dark shade of bronze. Her long-lashed eyes seemed at first glance to be as dark as midnight, but a closer look revealed traces of gray in them. Just by stepping out of the coach, she had caught the eyes of every man nearby—and held them.

So much so, in fact, Longarm realized with a start, that he hadn't even noticed the other three hombres who had gotten off the coach. Two of them he figured for Don Alfredo's assistants, just as Quine and Markson had come along to help out Franklin Barton. The other man wore the uniform of a *federale,* and the sight of it made Longarm tense. He had had more than his share of unfriendly run-ins with the Mexican federal police. But they were in Texas now, not Mexico, and besides, this *capitan* was here on a diplomatic mission, not to cause trouble.

For a few minutes, Longarm and Coffin were busy supervising the unloading of baggage from both coaches. Some of the idlers who were standing around watching were more than happy to earn a couple of dollars unloading the bags and taking them upstairs in the hotel. Longarm and Coffin made sure that each bag went to the proper room. Longarm figured it would be prudent not to let Coffin anywhere near Sonia's room, so he saw to that one himself. He was going to have to have a talk with the Ranger about proper behavior.

Hell, he understood how Coffin felt, though. One look at Sonia and he had wanted to fling her down right there in the street, pull her skirts and petticoats up over her head, and go at her in front of God, her father, and everybody else in Del Rio. And Sonia had looked as if she wouldn't have minded if he had done just that.

Maybe he was mistaken, he told himself sternly. Maybe she was just a nice, innocent Mexican gal with nothing on her mind but accompanying her papa on this trip to Texas.

But then he stepped into her room with his arms full of

her bags, and she turned toward him from where she was standing beside the bed, and it was all he could do not to drop the bags and jump her right then and there. She had taken off the jacket of her traveling outfit, revealing a lacy white silk blouse. Her heavy breasts thrust out proudly against the soft fabric, and he could plainly see her nipples through the silk. They were large and dark, and he could almost taste the sweet-salty tang of the pebbled flesh on his tongue.

"You are so kind, Señor Long," she said as Longarm set the bags on the floor. "My father has spoken much of you, of how your courage and daring saved him from a dreadful fate."

"Like I told him downstairs, it was sort of by accident," said Longarm. "I was just glad I was in the right place at the right time."

"Still, I am grateful." She moved closer to him, not stopping until she was only about a foot away. "Sometime, I would enjoy showing you just how grateful I am, Señor Long."

Well, thought Longarm, there wasn't much chance of misinterpreting *that* comment. Not with the way she was standing there looking up at him from heavy-lidded eyes, with her full red lips open just a little so that he could see the tip of her tongue. If she had leaned a little closer to him, her breasts would have been brushing his chest, and for one wild instant, Longarm considered closing that gap. It would have been so easy to slip his arms around her and pull her unresisting body tight against his.

Then a footstep in the hall reminded him that the door was still open, and he stepped back with a polite nod. "We'll have to see about that, señorita," he said. He touched a finger to the brim of his hat. "Enjoy your stay in Del Rio."

Then, before her charms could hypnotize him again, he turned away quickly and left the room.

The *federale* captain was standing in the hall, as if he was waiting there for Longarm. It turned out that he was, because as soon as Longarm shut the door of Sonia's room behind him, the Mexican officer nodded curtly to him and said, "I would speak with you, señor."

"All right," Longarm said coolly. "I'll be glad to listen."

"You are the one who some of the people of my country call El Brazo Largo, are you not?"

"I've been called that a time or two when I was south of the border," admitted Longarm.

The *federale*'s hatchetlike face twisted momentarily in a sneer. "When you were south of the border interfering in Mexico's business, you mean."

Longarm forced himself to control his temper, and said calmly, "Any time I've crossed the Rio Grande, I've had a damn good reason to do it."

The Mexican shrugged. "I did not come here to argue about the past," he said. "I am Capitan Pablo Hernandez. Just like you, I have been given the job of seeing that the delegates from my country remain safe during these meetings."

"Figured as much," said Longarm.

"In addition, I have taken it upon myself to insure that Señorita Guiterrez, though not an official member of the party, also is safe."

"I want the same thing," Longarm assured the man. He gave in to a twinge of curiosity and went on. "Just why did the girl come with her father anyway?"

Hernandez's voice dropped to a hiss as he said, "Dios knows why the wildcat does any of the things she does."

"Wildcat, eh?" said Longarm with a grin. "Reckon you must've had some trouble with Señorita Guiterrez before now."

"She is a *puta*!" said Hernandez in a whisper. He was practically trembling with outrage. "That one thinks only of what is between her legs, and she cares little who satisfies her cravings, so long as they are satisfied often!"

Longarm liked to think he wasn't a crude man by nature. So he tried to tell himself that he was only looking for information that might affect his job as he lifted an eyebrow, grinned wickedly at Hernandez, and asked, "How often does she invite *you* into her bed, *Capitan*?"

"Never!" exclaimed Hernandez. He sounded more offended that Longarm would ask such a thing, instead of disappointed over the answer he was forced to give. "I want only for her to allow me to do my job, but everywhere we go I am forced to waste time extricating the señorita from one embarrassing situation after another! And does her father ever deny her the right to accompany him on his travels whenever the mood strikes her? His pure little *princesa?* No, of course not!"

Longarm held up a hand as Hernandez's tone began to rise from its formerly conspiratorial tone. He didn't want what the *federale* was saying to be overheard by the wrong person and cause any hard feelings that might only make Longarm's job more difficult. "Don't worry, *Capitan,*" he said. "You have my word that I'll keep an eye on the señorita."

"Is that *all* you will keep on her? I know how that witch can work her magic."

"There won't be any embarrassing situations on this trip," Longarm declared. "I can promise you that."

And he meant it. When and if he bedded Sonia Guiterrez, he would be discreet about it.

Hernandez relaxed a little. He had almost worked himself into a lather, Longarm thought, and his face was flushed. Hernandez inclined his head in a minuscule nod, then turned and stalked away down the hall. Longarm was a little surprised he hadn't clicked his heels together before he left.

Longarm turned to start in the other direction, and saw Lazarus Coffin watching him from the end of the corridor. Coffin was leaning on the railing next to the staircase landing. As Longarm reached him, he asked, "What was you and that little greaser jawin' about, Long?"

"Captain Hernandez had a few concerns," replied Longarm. "I put 'em to rest."

Coffin's eyes narrowed. "I'd like to put that gal to rest. She'd be rode hard and put up wet when I was through with her, I can tell you that."

"Just don't tell anybody else," Longarm said. "Don Alfredo seems to have a blind spot where his daughter is concerned."

"You mean he don't notice when she looks at ever' man she runs across like a she-dog in heat?"

Longarm sighed. "Evidently not."

"Then I reckon he's got more troubles than just wranglin' with ol' Franklin about how the border's goin' to run."

Someone cleared his throat behind Coffin. Longarm hadn't seen anyone approach due to the Ranger's size, but he should have heard the footsteps. Franklin Barton circled around Coffin as the big man turned around sharply. Barton could walk like an Apache, and Longarm wondered how a Washington diplomat had acquired that skill.

"Excuse me," Barton said dryly, "but if it's not too much trouble, *ol' Franklin* would like to ask you gentlemen a question. If I'm not interrupting your gossip, that is." His voice practically dripped scorn.

Longarm felt a surge of anger. He reined in his temper and asked, "What is it, Mr. Barton?"

"Just where am I supposed to conduct these meetings with the Mexican delegation?"

Longarm frowned. "Why, I reckon in your room or Don Alfredo's. The government reserved suites for both of you, so there should be plenty of room."

"Well, there's not. This is totally unacceptable. I need a room with a large table and plenty of chairs, so I and my associates and Don Alfredo and his associates won't be crowded. Our discussions will require the study of many maps and land abstracts and other documents."

Coffin pushed his sombrero back and scratched at his shaggy black hair. "Sounds like you're talkin' about the dinin' room downstairs."

Barton thought for a second, then nodded. "Yes, that *might* do," he said. "I'd have to study it first, of course."

"Wait just a minute," said Longarm. "If you take over the dining room, where are the rest of the hotel guests going to eat? Not to mention any folks from here in town who take their meals there."

"Well, that's not my problem, now is it?" Barton said coldly. "It's *your* job to provide whatever it takes to make these meetings a success, Marshal. A great deal is riding on the results.''

Longarm's jaw tightened, and he didn't say anything for a moment. Barton's callous attitude rubbed him the wrong way, and there were things about this whole setup that had bothered Longarm from the first—such as why the meetings were even necessary in the first place. He could understand why the United States and Mexico might have to parley every now and then concerning the border in New Mexico and Arizona and California. After all, the dividing line between the two countries there was purely imaginary. Here in Texas there was a damn river, for God's sake! The U.S. was on one side and Mexico was on the other, and if the river changed course, well, then, so did the border. It was that simple.

Longarm knew from experience, though, that nothing was ever that simple where the government was concerned, any government. Barton and Guiterrez would have to talk about it for a week, study this map and that map, this document and that document, advance first one proposal and then another, and maybe—if everyone on both sides was lucky—wind up coming to the same conclusion that anybody with a brain in his head could have seen right off.

With a sigh, Longarm said, ''All right. I'll talk to the hotel owner and see what we can work out. If you take over the dining room, though, it's going to be harder than ever to keep it a secret why you're here in Del Rio.''

''After the way both delegations arrived, I'd say our presence here is hardly a secret anyway,'' Barton replied. The same thing had occurred to Longarm, but Barton didn't seem worried about it. He started down the hall, saying over his shoulder, ''Let me know when everything's taken care of.''

Coffin glowered at the diplomat's retreating back and muttered, ''I'd like to put my boot right up where the sun don't shine. It might do that fella some good.''

''I doubt it,'' said Longarm. ''Chances are he'd just refer it to some committee for further study.''

Coffin glanced over at Longarm and broke into a grin. ''Hell, Long, you ain't so bad after all. We got off to a rough start, but you might do to ride the river with."

Longarm bit back the sarcastic comment he might have made about how Coffin's approval meant so much to him. Instead, he said, "I'll go find the owner of the hotel and break the news to him that he's about to lose his dining room—at least part of the time."

Chapter 6

That afternoon was one of the most frustrating in Longarm's memory.

The hotel manager didn't like it one bit, but he finally agreed to close down the dining room and turn it over to the diplomats. Longarm didn't tell the man exactly who Barton, Guiterrez, and the others were, of course, just intimated that they were all there on important government business and would appreciate some cooperation.

"I suppose the guests can go over to the Red Top and eat," the manager said with a sigh. "What do you think the chances are that I can get the government to reimburse the hotel for the money it'll lose while this is going on?"

"I wouldn't count on it," Longarm replied honestly.

A little later, he brought Barton, Quine, and Markson down to the dining room to have a look at it. Barton didn't appear any too happy as he said, "I suppose this will have to do. I doubt very seriously that there would be anything more appropriate here in this border town." He gestured at the tables covered with red-and-white checked cloths. "We can put some of these tables together to make a larger one. You'll see to that, won't you, Mr. Long?"

"Sure," said Longarm. He and Coffin might have to move

the tables around themselves, but if that was what it took, he supposed they didn't have much choice.

"Let me know when you have things ready," Barton said as he turned and headed toward the lobby. "I want to get started as soon as possible so that I can get back to Washington."

"Shouldn't I check with Señor Guiterrez and make sure these arrangements suit him too?" Longarm asked Barton's retreating back.

"Of course, of course," said Barton offhandedly, but Longarm knew he didn't really care if the arrangements suited Don Alfredo or not.

How the hell had a fella like that wound up working for the State Department? Longarm wondered. Barton was supposed to be a diplomat, but you sure couldn't tell it by the way he treated those he considered to be hired help.

Luckily, Don Alfredo was more reasonable. Trailed by Capitan Hernandez, the little banty rooster of a *federale,* he came downstairs at Longarm's request and looked at the dining room, nodding in satisfaction.

"This will do quite well, Señor Long," he said. "Though in truth the meetings could have been carried on upstairs if need be."

"No, that's all right," Longarm told him. "This is the way Mr. Barton wants it."

"Then that is the way he shall have it." Amusement glittered for a second in the Mexican diplomat's eyes. "I just hope he does not expect me to be as agreeable in every matter that may come up in our discussions."

Longarm figured there wasn't much chance of that. He had a feeling Don Alfredo was a shrewd negotiator. The fact that he couldn't seem to see how lusty his daughter was didn't mean he wasn't sharp as a tack in other areas.

When Guiterrez had returned to his suite, Longarm and Coffin saw to arranging the tables the way Barton wanted them. Then Longarm headed for Barton's room, intending to inform the diplomat that everything was ready downstairs.

He was met in the second-floor corridor by Jeffery Spooner, who said sharply, "I want to talk to you, Mr. Long."

Everybody wanted to talk to him, thought Longarm, which really meant they wanted to issue demands or complain about something. He kept his tone carefully neutral as he asked, "What is it, Lieutenant?"

"It's Major," said Spooner in a half whisper. "And don't forget, Long, these are supposed to be *secret* meetings. You'd better call me Mr. Spooner."

With an effort, Longarm was able to keep from rolling his eyes in disgust. The way things had gone so far, nothing about the whole affair was going to be a secret for very long. "What do you need, Mr. Spooner?" he asked.

"I've heard that there was some trouble here early this morning, before we arrived. Is that true?"

Longarm nodded. "It is. A gang of outlaws raided the town and robbed the bank. Some of the citizens were killed in the shooting, and so were some of the bandits."

Spooner looked at him incredulously. "And yet you intend to let these meetings go on as if nothing has happened?"

"What else am I supposed to do?" asked Longarm. "That raid didn't have anything to do with what brought you here, Major. The fella who's ramrodding those desperadoes just decided to hit the town for a change, instead of another of the ranches around here. The gang made a good haul, but they took some heavy losses. I don't reckon they'll be back."

"Can you guarantee that?" Spooner snapped.

"I can't guarantee anything," said Longarm. Then he thought, *Except that this job is going to be a pain in the ass.* He went on. "But I can tell you that it's likely we won't see El Aguila again while we're here in Del Rio."

"El Aguila," Spooner repeated. "I suppose that's this bandit chief you spoke of?"

"Yep. Coffin, that Texas Ranger who's helping me out, plans to help the local sheriff run the gang to ground once these meetings are over."

Spooner nodded slowly. "Well, I suppose you know what you're talking about. I've heard that you're a good man at your job."

"I try," Longarm said dryly.

"So do I, Mr. Long. You should remember that."

''I will,'' said Longarm. ''Now, I need to tell Mr. Barton that everything's ready downstairs.''

''I'll do that,'' Spooner volunteered. ''Why don't you inform the Mexican delegation?''

Longarm nodded. ''All right.'' He stepped across the hall to Don Alfredo's door and rapped on it as Spooner went back into the American suite.

Instead of the Mexican diplomat or one of his associates, Sonia Guiterrez opened the door to Longarm's knock. ''Señor Long!'' she said, her wide mouth curving in a sultry smile. ''It is so good to see you again.''

Longarm didn't point out that it had only been a little over an hour since he had left her in her room. Instead, he cleared his throat and tried not to think about the impact she made on his senses. ''Señorita Guiterrez, I need to speak to your father.''

Her full lower lip extended even more than normal in a pout. ''You did not come to see me?''

''Not this time,'' said Longarm.

''Well, then, perhaps another time you will. Another time soon.''

Longarm swallowed and found his throat dry. ''Maybe so.''

Sonia gave him another of those maddening smiles, then turned her head and called, *''Papacito.''*

A moment later Guiterrez appeared beside her, smiling broadly. ''Yes, my dear?'' He glanced at Longarm. ''Ah, Señor Long. I take it that everything is in readiness downstairs.''

''Yes, sir,'' said Longarm. ''I reckon you and Mr. Barton can get things under way just as soon as you're ready.''

''Excellent. *Gracias*, Señor Long.''

Don Alfredo didn't seem to be in any hurry to come down and get the meetings started. Longarm hesitated a moment, then asked, ''Should I tell Mr. Barton that you'll be downstairs in a few minutes?''

''Soon, Señor Long, soon. No need to rush these things.''

Longarm nodded as understanding dawned in his brain. Don Alfredo didn't intend to go downstairs until he was sure that Franklin Barton and the other Americans were already there, waiting for him. Longarm glanced across the hall at the door of Barton's suite. It was closed, and something about it told Longarm it would stay that way for a while. Barton would be thinking the same thing Don Alfredo was. Appearances were the only things that really mattered to these gents, and neither of them wanted to seem too eager to get started.

With a tug on the brim of his hat, Longarm nodded. "Well, then, whenever you're ready," he muttered, then backed away from the door. Sonia closed it, but not without another of those smoldering, heavy-lidded glances at which she was so expert.

Longarm sighed and went downstairs to wait.

"Hell, you coulda stayed in Denver and I coulda stayed in Austin," complained Coffin as he and Longarm sat at a small table in a corner of the hotel lobby. "We're about as much use here as tits on a boar hog."

Longarm couldn't find it in himself to disagree with the big Ranger. He and Coffin had been waiting all afternoon for the diplomatic meetings to begin, and so far everyone concerned was still upstairs, each side trying stubbornly to outwait the other.

"Maybe if we went up there with our guns out," Coffin went on, "we could make them fellas come down here and do their jobs. Might have to boot 'em in the rear end a time or two on the way, but—"

"We can't do that," said Longarm.

"Why in blazes not? That might take 'em down a notch or two and make 'em a whole heap more reasonable."

"And make them declare war on each other," Longarm pointed out gloomily.

A broad grin spread across Coffin's bearded face. "Well, at least that'd be somethin' happenin', wouldn't it?"

Longarm just grunted and didn't say anything. If this stalemate went on much longer, he might start giving some serious consideration to Coffin's suggestion.

That was when, as if they had timed it, Lewis Markson

and one of Don Alfredo's assistants appeared at the second-floor landing. Longarm could see the men from where he sat. For a long moment, they sized each other up without speaking, then Markson said something that Longarm couldn't hear. The Mexican gestured at the stairs, as if inviting the American to go first. Markson shook his head and stepped back slightly, indicating with a sweep of his own hand that the other man should precede him.

If they kept up that routine for very long, thought Longarm as he watched them, he was going to draw his gun and shoot both of them. Coffin looked as if he felt the same way.

Finally, both men came down the stairs side by side and went to the arched entrance of the dining room. Longarm and Coffin sat up straight and watched as Markson and the Mexican looked around the dining room. A few more low-voiced comments and nods were exchanged, then the men turned and went back across the lobby to the staircase.

"Wait a minute," Longarm called in a strangled voice as he came to his feet. "Are you fellas about to get started or what?"

Markson smiled humorlessly at him. "Presently, Mr. Long, presently."

Coffin growled, "I'll presently your ass, you little—"

Longarm put a hand on the Ranger's shoulder as Coffin started to surge to his feet. "All right," he said to Markson, "but tell Mr. Barton that the sooner we get all this done, the better."

"Not necessarily," Markson replied blandly, then joined his companion from south of the border in ascending the stairs.

Coffin settled back in his chair. "I ain't cut out for this," he said between clenched teeth.

"Neither am I, old son," Longarm told him. "Neither am I."

Eventually, Barton and Don Alfredo both emerged from their suites and met at the top of the stairs, going through the same pointless exercise as their assistants had before coming down the staircase side by side. The other members of both delegations trooped along behind. Longarm and Coffin were waiting for them, and led the way into the dining room. When everyone was assembled—the Americans on one side of the tables that had been pushed together to make one big table, the Mexicans on the other—Franklin Barton turned to Longarm and Coffin and said, "Thank you, gentlemen. That will be all."

Longarm frowned. "I figured we'd sit in on the meetings, just to make sure there's no problem."

Barton shook his head emphatically. "Impossible. The things that will be said here are secret."

"You mean you don't trust us?" Coffin burst out.

Barton smiled and said, "I mean, Mr. Coffin, that you and Mr. Long have done your jobs. Now let us do ours."

Longarm supposed the diplomat had a point, though he was reluctant to admit it. He took hold of Coffin's arm and said, "Come on."

The Ranger jerked free. "Wait just a dang-blasted minute! He's sayin' we ain't good enough to hear what they got to say!"

"And I'm saying that as long as nobody bothers them, the rest of it ain't any of our business," Longarm pointed out. He lowered his voice and leaned closer to the Ranger as he went on. "Forget it, Coffin. You know it'd just be a bunch of political bullshit anyway."

"Yeah, I reckon you're right." Coffin allowed Longarm to steer him toward the door.

Longarm looked back at Barton and Don Alfredo. Their assistants were already opening leather portfolios and hauling out sheaves of paper. "One of us will be out in the lobby if you need us."

Both of the chief diplomats nodded. Barton said, "Thank you, Mr. Long," and Guiterrez added, "*Muchas gracias.*" Barton told Quine to shut the doors, and a moment later the entrance was closed, leaving Longarm and Coffin on the outside.

Longarm considered the situation. The single large window in the dining room was boarded up, having been shattered by outlaw bullets that morning. That left two ways into the room, the lobby entrance and the door into the kitchen, which could also be reached from a rear hallway. "You want to go sit in the kitchen or wait out here?" he asked Coffin.

The Ranger's brow furrowed in thought, then abruptly smoothed as an idea came to him. "You reckon that blond waitress from this mornin' might be back yonder in the kitchen?"

"She might be," replied Longarm, although he figured it was sort of doubtful.

"And the cook will be for sure, so I might could get me a little snack whilst I was standin' guard." Coffin nodded, as much to himself as to Longarm. "I'll take the kitchen."

"Fine by me," said Longarm. He headed back to the chair where he had been sitting before as Coffin shambled off toward the rear of the hotel.

Longarm paused long enough to get a cheroot burning, then settled down in the chair to wait some more. He kept his eyes fastened on the closed doors that led into the dining room and hoped he wouldn't doze off from sheer boredom.

There wasn't much chance of that, because a few minutes later Sonia Guiterrez came downstairs.

Longarm saw movement from the corner of his eye and glanced toward the staircase. Sonia was walking down the stairs, her hand trailing lightly on the polished banister. She had taken down her hair so that it fell in rich bronze waves around her head and shoulders, and had traded the traveling outfit she had worn earlier for a cinch-waisted gown with a neckline that swooped low enough to reveal the deep valley between her honey-colored breasts, which moved enticingly with each step she took down the stairs.

She left little doubt that she had come in search of Longarm. Her dark-eyed gaze fastened on him, and she came straight across the lobby toward him as he stood up. "Señor Long," she greeted him.

He nodded to her. "Señorita. What can I do for you?"

"Well . . . you could take me and make mad, passionate love to me so that my cries of ecstasy rise to the heavens and my fingernails leave the tracery of desire on your back."

Longarm swallowed and said, "Beg pardon, ma'am?" He

was glad she had pitched her voice so low that only he could hear it. The lobby was deserted except for the desk clerk, but Longarm didn't want that fella hearing what Sonia was saying.

She smiled wickedly and said, "Or perhaps you can just take me to dinner." She gave a dainty shrug that made her breasts do interesting things again. "Whatever you like."

Longarm shook his head. "It ain't a matter of what I'd like, Señorita Guiterrez. I'm afraid I have a job to do, and I can't abandon it."

"You mean guarding my father and the others while they conduct their tiresome meetings?" She sighed. "Surely your friend can do that? The big ugly man who calls himself Coffin?"

"Ranger Coffin has his own chores to attend to," Longarm told her. "I'm sorry, but I just can't leave right now."

"Are you certain?" Sonia leaned closer to him, and in a voice as sweet and thick with desire as molasses, she whispered, "After we have eaten, I would love to take your manhood and lick it slowly from one end to the other before I take it into my mouth and—"

"The Red Top Cafe across the street is a good place for supper," Longarm broke in harshly, knowing that he couldn't listen to much more of what Sonia was saying without beginning to show some evidence of his arousal. Under the circumstances, having the front of his trousers poking out didn't much appeal to him. He moved back a little so that the delicious, intoxicating scent of her wouldn't fill his nostrils quite so much, and then he went on. "I'm afraid the hotel dining room is closed for the time being."

He saw a flash of anger in her eyes, but it lasted only a moment. Clearly, she wasn't accustomed to having her offers turned down. However, the fact that Longarm was able to do so must have amused her, because she chuckled. "As you wish, Señor Long," she said. "But sooner or later . . . you will do as I wish. It is as inevitable as the rising of the sun." She glanced down at his groin. "Among other things."

"Yes, ma'am," said Longarm.

She turned and started to walk away, her hips swaying

provocatively, then paused and looked back at him over her shoulder. "Will you watch me to make certain I reach the cafe safely?"

"I reckon I can do that," replied Longarm with a nod. He figured he wouldn't be the only man watching her as she crossed the street. Every male eye in Del Rio within seeing distance would be fastened on her.

And he was afraid she was right. He was only human, and sooner or later he would succumb to her charms if she kept offering them that freely. Doing his job well was the most important thing in life to him.

But damn it, that didn't mean he was made of stone.

He watched her until she had crossed the street and entered the Red Top, then took his hat off and sleeved sweat from his forehead. Turning, he saw that the desk clerk was watching him. The fella had a sheen of sweat on his forehead too, and Longarm figured it wasn't from the border heat.

Longarm hoped Franklin Barton and Don Alfredo could settle things soon. He was afraid that if he had to stay in Del Rio for very long, Sonia Guiterrez would wind up killing him.

One way or another.

Chapter 7

The meeting in the hotel dining room went on until after dark. Longarm's belly began to growl, and he was glad when Coffin wandered out of the kitchen and offered to trade places with him for a while. Since Sonia Guiterrez had already come back to the hotel—giving Longarm a teasing, maddening smile as she walked up the stairs—Longarm figured it would be safe enough to leave Coffin on duty in the lobby. He wouldn't have if there had been any chance that Coffin might wind up alone with Sonia.

Of course, he was being a little hypocritical, he thought as he went back to the kitchen. He couldn't blame Coffin for wanting to take Sonia to bed when that was exactly what he intended to do himself as soon as he got the chance. Provided he could be discreet about it, naturally.

The cook was an elderly Italian man who jabbered incessantly at Longarm as the lawman ate. The man's words were a mixture of drawled English and rapid-fire Italian, and after a while the chatter made Longarm's head hurt a little. He finished up the steak and potatoes and beans and drank the last of the coffee in his cup. "Much obliged," he said as he got to his feet. The cook said something in Italian, so Longarm just smiled and nodded and went out.

Coffin looked up from the chair where he was slouched and said, "Don't send me back in there with that little Eye-talian fella, Long. I ain't a man to beg, but he like to drove me to distraction with all that jawin'."

Longarm took out a cheroot. Before he could say anything, the doors of the dining room opened, and Barton and Don Alfredo emerged, smiling and laughing. It looked as if the meeting had gone well.

"We're finished for the day, Mr. Long," Barton told Longarm, "and we're going up to our suites. Can you have some dinner sent up for us?"

Longarm nodded. "I'll see to it," he said. That would mean dealing with the talkative little Italian, but he figured he could manage that much.

"You boys get everythin' straightened out?" Coffin asked hopefully.

"We made a good start, señor," replied Guiterrez. "But there is much yet to discuss before a final agreement is reached."

Coffin did a poor job of suppressing a groan. Longarm felt the same way. But it was too much to hope that a few hours of talking could settle anything between two countries. Even if things had been that simple, no diplomat worth his salt would ever admit such a thing.

Barton and Guiterrez led the way upstairs, followed by their associates. Longarm told Coffin to station himself on the second-floor landing so that he could keep an eye on the corridor, then went back to the kitchen to see about getting some food for the diplomatic parties.

An hour later, when everyone had eaten, Longarm and Coffin found themselves standing alone on the landing. "Reckon they're down for the night," said Coffin. "Let's you and me go over to Kilroy's and get us a drink, Long."

Longarm shook his head. "One of us has to stay here all night. We'll trade off shifts, just like we were standing watch on the trail."

Coffin glowered at him and demanded, "You mean we got to ride night herd on these rannies too?"

Longarm shrugged and nodded. Coffin sighed heavily.

"You go ahead," he told Longarm. "I reckon I can wait."

"I'll relieve you at midnight."

"Don't you forget," Coffin warned.

Longarm gave him a grin and a casual wave as he strode down the stairs. A moment later he stepped out onto the boardwalk in front of the hotel and took a deep breath. The air was still hot from the day just past, and wouldn't really start to cool off until well after midnight. But at least he wasn't cooped up inside any longer.

The saloon was busy, with most of the tables occupied and men standing two deep at the bar in places. Most of the talk that Longarm heard as he made his way across the room was about the bandit raid on the town that morning. After dealing with Barton, Don Alfredo, and the others all day, the battle with El Aguila's gang seemed further in the past to Longarm than a mere fourteen hours or so. He spotted a gap at the bar and slid himself into it smoothly.

"Rye," Longarm said to the bartender, who came over to see what he wanted. "Tom Moore, and don't tell me you ain't got any, because you did last night." The words came out sharper than he intended, but he had a powerful thirst.

"Sure, Mr. Long," the bartender replied as he reached for a bottle and a glass.

"You're a man who knows what you want."

The deep, resonant voice came from beside Longarm. He glanced over and saw a man about the same height as he was, with the broad shoulders and narrow hips of a horseman. The stranger wore a broad-brimmed black hat and had a bright red bandanna tied around his tanned throat. A blue work shirt, denim trousers, scuffed boots, and chaps that bore the scratches of a lot of brush completed his outfit—along with crossed cartridge belts that supported a pair of holstered Colts with black grips. The man's face was too rugged to be called handsome, but there was power in the smoky-eyed gaze he turned toward Longarm. His wide mouth, which relieved slightly the prominence of his nose and jaw, was grin-quirked at the corners.

"I've got a fondness for Maryland rye," Longarm admitted. He felt a grudging respect for this stranger, but no liking.

"Man who knows his priorities has a leg up on the rest of us," said the stranger. He drained the last of the beer in the mug in his left hand, then set it down and used the same hand to take a coin from the pocket of his shirt. His right hand, with long, slender fingers, rested easily on the bar, not far from the butt of the gun on that side. The way the man used his left hand was enough to tell Longarm a great deal. Longarm had sort of the same habit himself.

This was a gent who knew how to use a gun—and quite frequently did just that.

But as long as he was peaceable, that was all that mattered to Longarm tonight. He sipped the drink that the bartender placed in front of him, then said to the stranger, "Buy you another beer?"

The man shook his head. " 'Fraid I've reached my limit. *Adios, amigo.*" With that, he turned and headed for the batwing doors of the saloon. Longarm watched him in the long mirror behind the bar. The stranger didn't shoulder anybody out of the way, but a path seemed to clear for him through the crowd anyway.

When the man had stepped out into the night and disappeared, Longarm inclined his head toward the door of the saloon and asked the bartender, "You know that fella?"

The bartender shook his head. "Never saw him before tonight. Looked to me like he might have been trouble, though, so I'm glad he's gone. We don't need no gunfighting drifters in here."

Before Longarm could say anything else, a soft hand laid itself on his arm, and he felt the unmistakable pressure of a woman's breast against his side. "Hello, Custis," said the redheaded Anna Marie.

Longarm turned his head and grinned down at her. "Hello, darlin'," he said. "You miss me?"

Her fingers squeezed his arm, and Longarm could feel their warmth through the sleeve of his shirt. "Of course I did. I thought about you very much today, Custis." She tilted her head, and her green eyes looked quickly around the room. "Lazarus, he is not with you?"

"Nope," Longarm said with a shake of his head. "He's

over at the hotel.'' He stopped short of explaining that Coffin was working at the moment. That was none of Anna Marie's business—though no doubt most of the townspeople were already gossiping about the arrival of the strangers from north and south and the closing down of the hotel dining room. The citizens of Del Rio might not know exactly what was going on, but by this time they knew that *something* was.

Anna Marie leaned closer to Longarm, molding her body to his in places. And soft, enticing places they were too, thought Longarm. Anna Marie said, ''Good. Then we can finish what we started last night when Lazarus interrupted us, no?''

''Seems to me like we finished, all right, just elsewhere,'' Longarm pointed out.

''Do not make fun of me, Custis,'' Anna Marie said sternly. ''Just come with me now.'' Once again, she tugged him toward the stairs.

Longarm tossed off the drink of rye and put the empty glass on the bar, then allowed her to lead him over to the staircase. No one stopped them this time as they climbed to the second floor. Anna Marie took him down the hall and stopped in front of a closed door.

''This is my room,'' she said unnecessarily.

''I'd like to see it,'' Longarm told her.

She hesitated. ''It is not a fancy place.''

''Neither was my hotel room. It's what two people do there that makes a place special.''

She smiled at that, and came up on her toes to press her mouth against his. Longarm felt her tongue darting against his lips, and opened them so that she could probe wetly into his mouth. His arms went around her waist and pulled her to him. The softness of her belly pressed against his groin, and she wiggled a little as she felt the prod of his stiffening shaft.

When Longarm took his mouth away from hers a moment later, he said in a husky voice, ''I reckon we'd better go on inside.''

Anna Marie was a little breathless as she replied, "Yes. I think that would be wise."

She reached behind her and turned the knob. As the door of the room swung open, Longarm tensed slightly. He had been led into more than one trap by a beautiful woman. But a lamp was already burning on the small table beside the bed, and the room was small enough so that he could see most of it from the hallway, could see that it appeared to be empty. He was cautious as he stepped inside, holding her right hand with his left. His right hovered close to the butt of his Colt. But as he closed the door behind him with his foot, he saw that the room was indeed empty except for the two of them. The bed, the small table, a chair, and a wardrobe with both doors open were the only items of furniture in the room. The wardrobe was stuffed full of frilly, lacy, feathery dresses. Somebody could have been hiding behind them, but when Longarm glanced at the bottom of the wardrobe, he didn't see any feet lurking there.

She must have sensed his suspicions, because she asked, "What is wrong, Custis?"

"Nothing," he told her. "Old habits die hard, I reckon. I'm a careful man. That's how I've stayed alive this long."

"Not too careful, I hope." She came into his arms again and ran her hand over his groin. "A man must be daring when he makes love. Are you daring, Custis?"

"Try me," he said in a mock growl as his embrace tightened around her.

"I intend to."

She began undressing him. Longarm helped out by tossing his hat onto a nail by the door and unbuckling his gunbelt. He took his watch from its vest pocket too, artfully concealing the derringer on the other end of the chain as he placed it on the chair underneath his vest. Anna Marie unbuttoned his shirt, tugging it from his trousers. As she bared his chest, she ran her fingers through the thick mat of dark brown hair that grew there. Then she reached down to his waist and went to work on his belt and the buttons of his fly. He was fully erect by now, and the tautness of the fabric at his crotch made her fumble a little with the buttons. She got them unfastened and pushed the trousers down around his knees.

"Sit on the bed, and I will take off your boots," she instructed him.

Longarm complied, enjoying the view as she turned away from him, straddled each leg in turn, and bent over to tug his boots off. While she was in that position, he rested his hands on the firm cheeks of her backside and braced her. She wiggled her rump against his palms and gave a low, throaty laugh.

When his boots were off, she finished pulling his pants off as well, leaving him in the bottom half of a pair of long underwear. Longarm stretched out on the bed and lifted his hips so she could peel those off him. His shaft sprang proudly upright, saluting her. She perched on the edge of the bed next to him and used both hands to stroke his manhood, sliding her palms down the thick pole of male flesh. Longarm gritted his teeth as a pang of pure pleasure pulsed through him. There was something very erotic about lying there completely naked while a lovely, fully dressed woman sat beside him playing with his rod.

"Why don't you get your clothes off?" he asked huskily after a moment.

"I will do that," said Anna Marie. With a final squeeze of his shaft, she stood up and began undressing. Longarm watched in admiration as each of her garments fell away from her, revealing the big-bosomed body he had enjoyed so much the night before. When she was naked, she came back to the bed and sat down beside him once more.

She leaned over his midsection, and for a second he thought she was going to take his manhood into her mouth. But then she filled her hands with her breasts and wrapped the soft, creamy globes of flesh around his shaft. She worked them back and forth, creating an exquisite sensation that drew a groan from his mouth.

"You like that, Custis?" she said with a maddening smile. "I can continue if you like."

"You do . . . whatever you want, darlin'," Longarm managed to say.

She straightened a little and put her hands on his thighs. Her fingers dug in with surprising strength and began kneading and massaging. She worked on the front of his legs for a few minutes, then told him to lift his knees. Longarm pulled his legs up so that she could rub the back of them. That also allowed her easy access to the fleshy sacs below his shaft. She cupped them in one hand, rolling them very gently from side to side.

While she was doing that, she leaned over and sent her tongue swooping several times around the head of his shaft. Then she kissed down the iron-hard length of him, and finally took the sacs in her mouth as well, using her hands to caress the muscles in the backs of his legs as she did so. Her red hair tickled the insides of his thighs.

Longarm reached for her hips and started to pull her around so that he could return the favor while she continued her French lesson on him. Instead she stopped him, grabbed one of the pillows, and placed it at the foot of the bed. Kneeling on all fours so that her backside was high in the air and facing Longarm, she rested her head on the pillow and said in a voice strained with passion, "Take me now, Custis. Any way you want, just . . . take me!"

Longarm gazed for a moment at the full, round cheeks of her bottom and the tempting cleft between them. Then, lifting himself on his knees and grasping his manhood so that he could guide it into her, he said, "I reckon the usual way is plenty good for me." With a surge of his hips, he sheathed himself in her hot, drenched depths.

From this angle, he was able to fill her as never before, and she gave a low cry and clutched at the pillow with her hands as he drove into her. "Oh! Oh! Oh, my God, Custis!" she gasped. "You are so big!"

Longarm had launched into a steady rhythm right away. He pistoned in and out of her, and with each surge forward, her muscles clamped tightly around him, releasing him only reluctantly as he withdrew. Then he thrust again, the long, thick pole throbbing as it delved deeply within her. She started to pant, and her hips jerked back and forth in a frenzy.

The minutes stretched out, seemed to become hours. Longarm was in complete control now, reveling in the pleasure he brought to her even as similar waves swept over him. He held tightly to her hips, his thumbs pressing into the globes of her bottom, steadying her so that her urgent movements wouldn't cause him to slip out of her. Deeper and deeper he drove, each thrust opening her up more and more. Heated flesh slapped against heated flesh, punctuating the harsh breaths, the soft, sharp cries that came from both of them.

His breath hissing between clenched teeth, Longarm pulled her against him and held her there while he shifted around on the bed. He stepped off so that he could brace his feet on the floor, then began thrusting even harder and faster. Anna Marie balled her hands into fists and struck the mattress as she practically sobbed in a delirium of ecstasy.

Finally, there was no way either of them could continue. As her hips pushed back against him, Longarm tightened his grip on her and drove himself full-length inside her. His seed began to burst from him in long, shuddering spasms. Anna Marie made a high, keening sound as her own climax gripped her. Longarm emptied himself into her, giving a couple of small, involuntary jerks as the last drops were milked from him.

Longarm would have withdrawn from her slowly, but she collapsed as if all her bones had turned to jelly, slumping down on the bed and hugging the pillow to her as if she never intended to let go of it. Her smooth back rose and fell dramatically as she gasped for breath and tried to recover from the storm of passion that had overwhelmed her. Longarm slid down onto the bed beside her, reclining on his stomach as she was doing.

Anna Marie turned her head so that she could see him. There were tears in her bright green eyes. "Custis, you are . . . you are like no man I have ever met!"

In her line of work, she had probably said that same exact thing to plenty of men, so Longarm took it with a grain of salt. She must have seen the doubt in his eyes, because she lifted herself on her elbows and went on quickly, "No, I mean it! You have brought me so much joy, so much . . . I cannot find the words!"

Longarm put a hand behind her head, burying his fingers in the thick, red hair, and pulled her closer to him. "I know what you mean," he said quietly, then brushed his lips across hers.

Anna Marie put her hand on his jaw and kissed him harder. Longarm would have thought it unlikely, if not impossible under the circumstances, but he was convinced he felt a slight stirring in his groin again.

He broke the kiss and twisted around so that he could bend over the lamp on the bedside table and blow it out. Darkness fell over the room and brought with it silence, broken only sporadically by giggles, moans, and the soft, sibilant sound of flesh on flesh.

For a couple of hours, Longarm didn't even think about the job that had brought him to Del Rio.

Chapter 8

Unfortunately, midnight rolled around all too soon, so Longarm wasn't able to spend the night sleeping in Anna Marie's arms. He had to get up and go over to the hotel, where Lazarus Coffin was waiting anxiously to be relieved of guard duty.

"I got to get me a drink," said the big Ranger as he started down the stairs. "You need me, I'll be over at Kilroy's."

Longarm was glad that Coffin didn't mention the red-headed saloon girl. He didn't want any more trouble over her with Coffin—but at the same time, he wanted Anna Marie to be able to spend the night dreaming about *him*.

That thought brought a wry grin to Longarm's face. Deep inside every man, he supposed, no matter how old the fella was, there was a half-grown boy who still wanted to think that any gal he kissed was going to dream about him. In this case, it was about as likely as a longhorn sprouting wings and flying away . . . but the feelings were there inside Longarm anyway.

"Be here by six o'clock," he warned Coffin.

The Ranger stopped halfway down the staircase and glared back up at Longarm. "Why the hell so early?" demanded Coffin.

"For one thing, I'm liable to want some breakfast by then. For another, we don't know what time these fellas are going to get started again."

Coffin shrugged his acceptance and went on down the stairs and out of the hotel lobby, grumbling all the way. Longarm sat down in the chair that Coffin had been occupying until recently.

The rest of the night passed quietly and peacefully. Longarm still would have preferred spending it in Anna Marie's bed, rather than dozing in a chair in a second-floor hotel corridor. But morning eventually came, and with it Sheriff Sanderson.

The local lawman trotted up the stairs as Longarm was standing and stretching stiff muscles. "Mornin'," Sanderson greeted him. "Any trouble last night?"

"Not around here," replied Longarm. "Heard anything about El Aguila's bunch?"

"Nobody in these parts has seen hide nor hair of 'em since that little set-to early yesterday mornin'. And that's all right with me."

"Seen Coffin? He's supposed to be here any time to relieve me."

Sanderson frowned. "Is that right? Well, then, I reckon I'd better go back down the street and let him out of jail."

"Jail!" exclaimed Longarm. "You've got him locked up?"

"Seemed like the thing to do at the time. Otherwise he was bound and determined to bust up Kilroy's place. He was mad 'cause that redheaded gal won't have anything to do with him anymore."

Longarm bit back a groan. Trouble had cropped up after all, even though he hadn't been aware of it. "When did this happen?"

" 'Bout one o'clock in the mornin'." Sanderson yawned and scraped a hand over the bristles on his jaw and chin. "Must be why I'm so tired this mornin'. Spent too much of the night rasslin' that big buffalo into a jail cell."

Longarm was surprised Sanderson had been able to arrest Coffin by himself. The Ranger would have made almost two of the sheriff. Obviously, Sanderson was tougher than he looked. Either that, or Coffin had held back out of respect for the local star-packer. That seemed unlikely . . . but then, Coffin was something of a contradiction to start with.

"Sorry I didn't hear the ruckus," Longarm told Sanderson.

"It don't matter none. You couldn't have come over to give me a hand, even if you had. Now could you?"

Longarm glanced down the hall at the closed doors of the suites housing the diplomatic parties. "No, I reckon not."

"I figured as much. Don't worry about it, Marshal. I handled ol' Lazarus all right. Don't forget, I got plenty of experience at it. That boy's been raisin' hell around here for a long time." Sanderson started down the stairs. "I'll go turn him loose and tell him to get his sorry ass over here. That way you can go get a surroundin'."

"Much obliged, Sheriff," Longarm called after him.

Coffin showed up a quarter of an hour later, his face as dark with anger as a thunderhead. "I swear," he said as he came up the stairs, talking to himself as much as to Longarm, "one of these days I'm goin' to whup that little son of a bitch—"

"No, you won't," Longarm told him. "He's a lawman, and you are too, Coffin."

Coffin glared at him. "You never had to go up against a badge-toter in your time, Long?"

"Not an honest one," Longarm said, remembering a few crooked—not to mention homicidal—lawmen he had run into over the years. A badge didn't always mean a fella was on the same side as he was, but Longarm was usually willing to give the man the benefit of the doubt until he proved otherwise.

Coffin jerked a thumb at the stairs. "Aw, hell, go get your breakfast. I've already et."

"The sheriff fed you, huh?" Longarm couldn't resist asking as he started down the stairs. Coffin just glowered darkly at him.

By the time Longarm got back to the hotel, Coffin had already had breakfast sent up to the suites from the kitchen.

The little Italian cook wasn't happy about having to prepare food for such a small number of people, Coffin informed Longarm, but he was doing it.

"You reckon they'll finish up their jawin' today?" Coffin asked hopefully.

"I'd be mighty surprised if they did," said Longarm.

They didn't. Three more days rolled by, in fact, and although Franklin Barton and Don Alfredo Guiterrez both seemed optimistic that an agreement would be reached soon, Longarm couldn't tell if they were getting any closer to being finished. Though Barton got along well with Don Alfredo, he was as prickly as ever with Longarm, Coffin, and his assistants, constantly finding fault with nearly everything they did. The meals weren't right, the hotel beds were uncomfortable, the weather was too hot and dusty—and somehow Barton made all of that seem like Longarm's fault.

Longarm hoped these meetings wouldn't go on for too much longer. He would purely hate to have to wire Billy Vail in Denver with the news that he'd punched Franklin Barton right in his obnoxious face.

And then there was Sonia Guiterrez.

Longarm had never been one to be too upset when an attractive woman was interested in him, but Sonia was about to make him go plumb crazy. She seized every opportunity to rub up against him or make low-voiced comments about what she would like to do to him and what she wanted him to do to her. There was never any chance to act on her attempts at seduction, however, and after a while Longarm got the idea that was the way she wanted it. He was about to decide that she was one of those women who liked to get a fella all hot and bothered, all the while knowing that there wasn't a damn thing he could do about it.

He wondered if she was doing the same thing to Coffin. From the way he glared at her when she wasn't looking and muttered under his breath and clenched and unclenched his hands, Longarm figured she was.

But at least there had been no sign of El Aguila. Sheriff Sanderson was convinced that the bandit leader and his gang were still on the other side of the Rio Grande. As far as Longarm was concerned, they could stay there.

On the evening of his fifth full day in Del Rio, Longarm was strolling back across the street toward the hotel after eating dinner at the Red Top when he heard someone call softly from the mouth of an alley, "Señor Long."

Longarm stopped, recognizing Sonia's voice. She went on. "Please, Señor Long, I need you."

Longarm wasn't in the habit of walking into dark alleys, no matter how seductive the voice summoning him might be. That was a good way to wind up dead. Instead, he asked in a quiet voice, "What is it, Señorita Guiterrez?"

She came out of the alley mouth then, stepping into the light from a window that fell across the gap in the boardwalk. Longarm could see that she was unarmed.

Well, not exactly unarmed, he thought. The long red skirt and the white peasant blouse she wore concealed the real weapons she carried, but just barely. The neckline of the blouse was scandalously low. She looked like the sort of woman who ought to be in a cantina somewhere, dancing sensuously to the music of a guitarist, rather than the daughter of a wealthy, powerful diplomat.

Longarm walked toward her, still cautious, and she came to meet him. She caught hold of his left hand as she stepped up to him. "Señor Long, you have tormented me enough," she said.

"Tormented you?" said Longarm. "I figured it was the other way around."

"No! Day after day I have watched you and felt my need for you growing." She tugged him toward the alley mouth. "I would have you at last. No longer can I stand the tortures of desire."

She had a high-flown way of talking, that was for sure. Longarm allowed her to lead him into the alley. Maybe the time had finally come. It took only a moment for his eyes to adjust to the gloom of the alley, and he saw that they were alone.

Sonia came into his arms and lifted her mouth to his. Her kiss was searing as her lips pressed hard to his. Longarm put his arms around her and pulled her against him, feeling the soft cushions of her breasts flatten against his chest. He slid one hand down her back to the swell of her hips and caressed her bottom, squeezing hard on each cheek. She thrust her tongue between his lips, the tip of it fencing with his own.

After a moment, Sonia reached down to caress his manhood through his trousers. She broke the kiss and uttered a small cry of delight at the size of him. "Ah, Señor Long," she sighed, "you will fill me so well!"

"You intend for us to have at it right here in the alley?" Longarm asked her.

"Yes! Take me like you would a *puta*! That is what I am tonight, Señor Long. I am your whore."

Well, if that was what she wanted, thought Longarm, he supposed he ought to oblige her. It had been his experience that some women, even fancy ladies, liked to act anything but ladylike on occasion.

"Do it to me standing up," Sonia hissed as she reached down to hike up her long skirt. In the faint light that filtered into the alley, Longarm could barely see the smooth, straight columns of her bare legs. She spread her legs a little and leaned back against the wall of a building, her skirt up around her hips now so that he could see the thick forest of dark hair at the juncture of her thighs. She closed her eyes as she breathed hard and waited for him to ravish her.

Longarm was ready to do just that. His pole jutted out from his trousers as he undid the buttons. He stepped up between her spread legs and heard her crooning obscenities in Spanish under her breath. "Hard and fast, Señor Long," she whispered. "Take me hard and fast."

She was really something, thought Longarm. But he gave her what she wanted—hard and fast.

Her channel was wet and ready for him, and the feminine muscles clasped him in a hot, buttery grip as he filled her. "Yes, yes!" she chanted. Longarm thrust in and out of her, not bothering to try to delay anything this time. She was more than ready. She was, in fact, way ahead of him. He hadn't stroked into her more than half-a-dozen times when she began to spasm around him. Her hands grabbed his shoulders and hung on tightly as her climax shook her. Longarm kept driving into her, and each time his shaft socketed home, she gave a sharp little cry of passion.

He felt his own climax boiling up with an intensity that was surprising considering the short time he had been inside her. With Sonia Guiterrez, though, time didn't really mean much. A few minutes with her packed in all the desperate craving that might take an hour with most women. With a grunt of effort, Longarm slammed into her again, almost lifting her off her feet, and began spurting.

Sonia flung her arms around his neck and pulled his head down so that she could kiss him again. Longarm groaned as the last of his climax rippled and swept through him. Even though the lovemaking with Sonia had lasted only a few minutes, it had been every bit as good as Longarm had anticipated.

So good, in fact, that it was a few seconds before he heard the yelling and the gunshots over the pounding of the blood in his head.

But then the sounds penetrated his passion-numbed brain and caused him to jerk around, pulling out of Sonia's embrace. "What the hell!" Longarm exclaimed.

"Señor Long! What—"

The thunder of galloping hoofbeats came from the street. Longarm was already heading in that direction, buttoning up his fly as he hurried toward the sound of trouble. He palmed out his Colt as he came out of the alley mouth and bounded up onto the boardwalk.

Several riders were galloping along the street toward him. Bright orange muzzle flashes split the night, accompanied by the boom of shots. Over the racket, Longarm heard the yells of alarm. "El Aguila! El Aguila!"

"Damn it!" Longarm grated. The outlaw leader had come back after all. What was he after now, since he had already cleaned out the bank?

Longarm lifted his gun and squeezed off a shot at one of the galloping, shooting raiders. The darkness made for uncertain shooting, and he didn't think he hit anything. The shot drew the attention of the outlaws, however, and a second later Longarm was forced to dart back into the alley as a hail of owlhoot lead raked across the boardwalk where he had been standing.

"Señor Long!" Sonia screamed from somewhere down the alley, but there was no passion in her voice now, only fear.

"Stay back!" Longarm shouted at her. "Get back in the shadows and stay down!"

El Aguila's men pounded past the mouth of the alley. Longarm threw himself onto the ground, expecting them to throw more lead in his direction, but something else had already caught their attention and they were shooting at it. As the raiders swept past, Longarm scrambled back to his feet.

If the bandits were following the same pattern as before, they would make several passes through town before fleeing. Enough time had passed since the first raid for the banker to have replaced at least some of the stolen cash with more currency from the reserve bank in San Antonio, Longarm realized. Maybe that was what they were after.

He leaped back onto the boardwalk, hoping that Coffin would have the sense to stay where he was in the hotel and keep the members of the diplomatic parties there too.

Except for Sonia, of course. She had already slipped out of the hotel, so it was too late to do anything except hope that she would lie low until after the raid was over.

Longarm looked toward the far end of the street, where just as he had thought they would be, the outlaws were wheeling their horses for another swift gallop through Del Rio. This time Longarm was sure they were after something else, because simply shooting up the town wasn't going to gain them anything. He turned and ran toward the sheriff's office, thinking that he ought to join forces with Sanderson.

Before he could get there, he heard the crackle of more gunfire coming from the direction he was going. He had been right—the gang had split up, and while some of them were raising a deadly ruckus by riding up and down the street and shooting, the rest of the outlaws were up to some even more sinister purpose. Longarm ran harder as he saw muzzle flashes in the vicinity of the sheriff's office.

The outlaws were after Sanderson, he thought. They must have considered the lawman a threat, and now they were trying to get rid of him. Several men on horseback reared their mounts in front of the adobe building that housed the sheriff's office and jail and poured lead through the windows and the open door.

Longarm dropped into a crouch behind a rain barrel that was probably seldom used in this dry border country. It would give him some cover as he tried to catch El Aguila's men in a cross fire. Sanderson was already fighting back from inside the jail. Longarm heard the boom of a shotgun, and saw one of the outlaws slump in the saddle.

He lined his sights on another of the mounted figures and squeezed the trigger. The outlaw's hat flew off, and with a startled yell, he jerked his horse around so that he was facing Longarm. He fired the pistol in his hand, and Longarm ducked as slugs knocked splinters from the barrel.

"Forget him!" a voice boomed. "Get the sheriff!"

"This'll root him out of there!" shouted another member of the gang.

Longarm lifted his head and peered over the top of the barrel in time to see a stick of dynamite spinning through the air, trailing sparks from its furiously burning length of fuse. It disappeared through the open door of the sheriff's office as Longarm watched in horror.

A thunderclap split the night as the dynamite exploded and blew out what little glass remained in the windows of the building. Big chunks were knocked out of the adobe walls. Longarm grated a curse, knowing that Sheriff Sanderson had probably been killed by the blast.

Heavy footsteps thudded on the boardwalk behind Longarm. He whirled around, ready to fire, but his finger froze on the trigger as he saw Lazarus Coffin running toward him. "What the hell happened?" bellowed the big Ranger.

"El Aguila just blew up the sheriff's office!" Longarm shouted back. Then he jerked his gun up and triggered a shot practically in Coffin's face.

Coffin stumbled backward and yelped in surprise, but Longarm's bullet had already sizzled past his ear to bury itself in the chest of a mounted outlaw who had been drawing a bead on the Ranger's back. The desperado slid from his saddle and toppled lifelessly to the street. Coffin glanced over his shoulder at the corpse and grunted in appreciation of what Longarm had just done.

Longarm wasn't looking for any thanks. He snapped, "Get back to the hotel!"

"But—" Coffin began.

"Move, damn it!" ordered Longarm. "If those owlhoots go after Barton and the others for some reason—"

Longarm didn't have to finish the sentence. Coffin was already wheeling around and running toward the hotel, which was several doors away on the same side of the street.

Longarm's Colt held only two more bullets, and he fired them both at the outlaws who were still milling around in front of the dynamite-blasted sheriff's office. He ducked behind the barrel again as lead clawed the air around him. Desperately, he dumped the spent shells from the gun's cylinder and started thumbing in fresh cartridges.

"We got what we wanted!" shouted one of the outlaws. "Let's go!"

As Longarm had suspected, getting rid of Sheriff Sanderson had been the gang's goal in this raid tonight. Now, with the pounding of hoofbeats, they were fleeing once more. Longarm snapped the cylinder closed on the reloaded Colt and tensed, ready to raise up and open fire on the outlaws as they fled.

That was when he heard the very last thing he wanted to hear right now.

"Señor Long!" screamed Sonia Guiterrez.

Longarm twisted around and saw her stumbling toward him along the edge of the street. Behind her, bearing down hard, one of El Aguila's men was galloping straight toward her.

Chapter 9

Longarm flung his revolver up and fired, but the masked outlaw had already veered his horse to the side so that the bullet whipped harmlessly past him. He didn't intend to trample Sonia at all.

What he had in mind was even worse.

Sonia screamed again as the rider leaned down and grabbed her, looping an arm around her as he jerked her up off her feet. Longarm bit back a curse. He couldn't fire again, not with Sonia thrashing around in the man's grasp like that. There was a better than even chance he would hit her if he tried to make a fancy shot.

But that didn't mean he was going to let the son of a bitch just ride off with her. Jamming his Colt back in its holster, Longarm left the boardwalk in a desperate dive that he timed to intercept the outlaw as the man rode past.

Unfortunately, the owlhoot saw Longarm coming and kicked his left foot free of the stirrup. His leg came up and the heel of his boot slammed into Longarm's chest, catching the lawman in midair. Longarm was knocked backward, where he crashed into a hitch rack next to the boardwalk. All the breath was knocked out of him, and although he tried to maintain his balance, he slipped to his knees as he gasped for air. The only thing that kept him from falling on his face was the hitch rack, which he grabbed, reaching behind him, in an effort to stay upright.

The outlaw who had snatched Sonia was well past him now, racing on down the street to join the rest of the gang. Longarm pushed himself to his feet and drew his gun again, then gave another bitter curse as he realized he couldn't even try a shot at the fleeing outlaw's back. The .44 slug could easily tear through the man's body and strike Sonia. Longarm started looking around for a mount of his own. If a horse was tied nearby at one of the hitch racks, he could commandeer it and take off after the outlaws.

But all the horses that had been tied along Del Rio's main street had gone crazy and pulled their reins loose when they were spooked by the continuing volleys of gunfire. Longarm saw several broken reins still dangling from the thick poles that formed the racks. By the time he found a horse to ride, El Aguila's gang would be gone.

That didn't mean he couldn't pick up their trail, though. He turned and ran toward the closest livery stable, thinking that he could find a mount there.

Longarm's route took him toward the ruined sheriff's office, and just as he reached the building, a bloody, tattered figure reeled out through the half-destroyed doorway. Longarm leaped toward Sheriff Sanderson as the local star-packer began to collapse. He caught Sanderson under the arms and gently lowered him to the ground.

"I didn't expect to see you alive again after that dynamite blast, Sheriff," Longarm said grimly.

"I reckon I'm . . . about half dead," gasped Sanderson. His clothes were little more than bloodstained rags, and there were a couple of ugly gashes on his head that were still oozing crimson. He surrendered to a series of wracking coughs, his lungs no doubt full of smoke from the fire that was burning inside the office. When he was able to speak again, he rasped, "When I saw that . . . dynamite come in through the door . . . I jumped behind my desk as fast as I could. . . ."

Longarm recalled the sheriff's desk from his visit to the

office right after his arrival in Del Rio. It was an old, heavy piece of furniture, covered by nicks and scars and burned spots. But obviously, it had provided enough shelter to save the sheriff's life.

"Blast turned it over . . . on me," Sanderson went on. "Had a devil of a time . . . pushin' it off . . . 'fore the fire got me. Feels like my . . . left arm's busted."

Longarm glanced at the sheriff's arm, which was hanging crookedly from the shoulder, and agreed with Sanderson's diagnosis. But the local lawman was still alive, and that was more than he had any right to expect after having been so close to the blast.

Where were all the townspeople? Longarm asked himself as he looked around the street. El Aguila's gang was getting further away with every passing second—and Sonia Guiterrez was with them, held prisoner. Longarm needed someone to show up and take care of Sanderson so he could get started after the outlaws. The street was deserted, though. Everybody in town was hiding out until they were sure that the raid was over. Longarm supposed he couldn't blame them. They were ordinary citizens. Their job wasn't fighting bloodthirsty desperadoes like El Aguila's bunch.

But *his* job was to protect the members of the diplomatic parties who had come to Del Rio to negotiate, and since Sonia was one of them—albeit unofficially—he had failed.

Longarm didn't like to fail.

"Stay right here, Sheriff," he told Sanderson. "I'm sure somebody'll be along to tend to you pretty soon."

"Where else am I . . . goin'?" Sanderson asked. He looked up at the federal lawman who knelt beside him and blinked blood out of his eyes. "What's wrong . . . Marshal?"

"One of El Aguila's men grabbed Señorita Guiterrez."

Sanderson found the strength to exclaim, "Good Lord! How . . ."

"She was out in the street and one of those bastards grabbed her up from horseback," Longarm said. He didn't explain what Sonia had been doing out of the hotel in the first place.

Sanderson gripped his arm. "You got to . . . go after 'em . . . get her back . . ."

"That's just what I intend to do," Longarm promised him.

"Long!" The shout came from down the street. Longarm turned his head and saw Lazarus Coffin running toward them. The big Texas Ranger had the pearl-handled Remington revolver in his hand, but there were no longer any enemies to shoot at. All the outlaws had galloped out of Del Rio.

"I thought I told you to stay at the hotel," grated Longarm as Coffin pounded up.

"I tried, but that fella Don Alfredo's about half crazy out of his mind scared. Seems like his daughter ain't nowhere to be found, and he ordered me to come look for her."

Longarm nodded. "One of El Aguila's men got her."

"What? You mean she's dead?"

"Nope. Scooped up and carried off. Kidnapped."

"Shit!" Coffin said fervently. "This is turnin' into a bigger mess than I thought."

Amen to that, Longarm added silently.

"What do we do now?" Coffin went on. "We're goin' to chase after those owlhoots, aren't we?" He gestured at Sanderson. "And what happened to the sheriff here?"

"I damn near got . . . blowed up . . . you big ox," said Sanderson. "One of those raiders tossed . . . dynamite into the office."

Longarm got to his feet. "You look after the sheriff," he told Coffin. "I'm going to find a horse and get started after El Aguila's gang."

"You can't go by yourself," argued Coffin. "Hell, this is more my job than it is yours, since this is Texas and I'm a Ranger."

"Somebody want to . . . gimme a hand down to the doc's office?" asked Sanderson, interrupting the argument before it could get started good.

Longarm and Coffin both reached down and carefully lifted the sheriff to his feet. Sanderson slipped his uninjured right arm around Coffin's waist. "Come on, Lazarus," he said. "You can catch up to Marshal Long later."

Coffin grumbled and glowered, but he set up off the street toward the doctor's office, holding Sanderson upright and steadying the local lawman. Their progress was slow but steady.

Longarm turned and hurried toward his original destination, the closest livery stable. As he trotted through the open double doors, a voice that was quavery with fear called out, "Who's there? Don't move, mister, I got a gun on you."

Longarm hoped that wasn't true, because the owner of the voice sounded so spooked that he might shoot at anything without any warning or provocation. Holding his hands in plain sight, Longarm said, "I'm a lawman, a deputy United States marshal. I'm not looking for trouble. I just need to borrow a horse so that I can go after those men who just raided the town."

A short, stocky, balding man with tufts of white hair above each ear raised up from behind several bales of hay that had been stacked to one side of the stable. He didn't have a gun, as he had indicated earlier, but he was clutching the handle of a pitchfork with wickedly curving tines. They glittered in the light from a lantern that was hung on a nail in the wall nearby.

"A lawman, you say?" The stable man's voice was still reedy and nervous.

"That's right," said Longarm. "I can show you my badge and identification papers if you want."

The man shook his head. "No, I reckon that's all right. I've seen you around town with Sheriff Sanderson and that big galoot of a Ranger, so I suppose you must be telling the truth. You're going after those outlaws, you say?"

"That's right." Longarm didn't waste time explaining about how Sonia Guiterrez had been kidnapped. "Do you have a horse I can use?"

The man lowered the pitchfork. "Right over there," he said, pointing to one of the stalls. "That bay mare's a good horse. Need a saddle? Got a couple in the tack room."

Longarm's own saddle was back in his hotel room, and he didn't want to take the time to retrieve it. "Thanks," he grunted. "I'll take the saddle too."

"I'll get the best one I've got while you're putting a blanket on the mare," the stableman offered.

Within a few minutes, they had the bay mare ready to ride. Longarm swung up into the borrowed saddle, and found it not as comfortable as his own but passable. He nodded to the stable man, said, "Much obliged," and heeled the bay into a run that carried it out of the livery and into the street.

The outlaws had headed south, which came as no surprise to Longarm. He expected that they were fleeing across the border again. If anything had happened to slow them down, however, there was still a chance that he might be able to catch up to them before they reached the Rio Grande. As he galloped out of Del Rio, he could smell the haze of dust still floating in the air. That was an encouraging sign, an indication that he wasn't too far behind the outlaws.

There had been at least a dozen of them, and the tracks their horses had left were visible in the light of the moon and stars floating in the ebony sky overhead. The trail arrowed straight south, as Longarm had expected it would. He rode hard, but with each long stride of the bay, his spirits sank a little. It didn't take long to reach the river, and along the way he saw nothing except the tracks leading south.

"Damn it," he said aloud as he pulled the horse to a stop on the Texas side of the Rio Grande. The river was fairly wide here and ran between low sandy banks. The tracks leading into the stream were plain to see. Faintly, very faintly, Longarm could hear the pounding of hoofbeats from somewhere across the river. The sound faded away completely as he sat there seething.

Every instinct in his body, every fiber of his being, called out for him to ride across there and go after them. Under other circumstances, that was probably exactly what he would have done.

But back there a couple of miles in Del Rio, representatives of the U.S. and Mexican governments had been meeting to discuss this very border, and Longarm knew it would look bad for him to so flagrantly violate it as he was considering. If he crossed the Rio Grande, he would be alone over there, with no jurisdiction.

Of course, it wouldn't be the first time . . . and there was something else to consider—Sonia Guiterrez. She was the daughter of the head of the Mexican delegation. Surely that would carry some weight.

Still, the right thing to do, Longarm knew, was to turn around and go back to Del Rio so that he could find out how Don Alfredo wanted to proceed. Added to that was the fact that Longarm's job here in Texas was to protect the diplomats, not to go chasing after owlhoots, no matter who they might have kidnapped. Logically, he had to return to Del Rio, so he turned the bay around and prodded it into a ground-eating trot toward the town.

But it was still one of the hardest things he had ever done.

By the time he reached Del Rio, some of the citizens were on the street again, wandering around and looking dazed. Longarm had seen the same reaction during the war, in men who had been part of too many battles. These townspeople weren't used to being raided by bloodthirsty bandits and having to dive for cover at a moment's notice. They didn't care about the discussions between the U.S. and Mexico or the representatives of either side. All they wanted was for their lives to get back to normal.

Don Alfredo Guiterrez rushed out of the hotel as Longarm brought the horse to a stop in front of it. "Señor Long!" he exclaimed before Longarm could even begin to swing down from the saddle. "Did you find my daughter?" The tremble in Don Alfredo's voice made it clear that he was very afraid of the answer, whatever it might turn out to be.

"I didn't see any sign of her," Longarm replied honestly. He dismounted and looped the reins over the hitch rack, then turned once more to Don Alfredo. "It sure looked to me like El Aguila's bunch took her over into Mexico with them."

A string of Spanish curses exploded from Don Alfredo's mouth. The man was normally so dignified that to see him this frazzled made things seem even worse, thought Longarm. Don Alfredo clutched at his arm and asked, "Why would they take her? Why?"

Normally, Longarm didn't care for folks grabbing him like that, but he figured he could let it pass this time. Guiterrez was mighty shaken up, as well he should be. Longarm explained, "It looked to me like Sonia was just in the wrong place at the wrong time. One of those owlhoots saw her and decided on the spur of the moment to snatch her up. I think they came into town in the first place to try to kill Sheriff Sanderson."

Don Alfredo passed a shaking hand over his face. "The sheriff, he is all right?"

"As far as I know, he probably will be. He's got a busted arm and some cuts and bruises, but he's in pretty good shape for a man whose office was blasted with dynamite."

"*Dios mio,*" breathed Don Alfredo. "Are there any depths to which this El Aguila will not stoop?"

"There don't seem to be."

Don Alfredo clenched his right hand into a fist and pounded it into the palm of his left. "Sonia should not have been out of the hotel," he declared, anger warring now with the fear in his tone. "Who is responsible for that?"

"Reckon I am," Longarm said slowly, even though he had been away from the hotel at the time and Coffin had been supposed to keep an eye on things. "I'm responsible for the safety of your party, Don Alfredo, and I'm afraid I've let you down. That's why I want to cross the Rio Grande and try to get your daughter back from El Aguila's gang."

"No!" The sharp retort came from the door of the hotel. Captain Hernandez, the little *federale,* stepped out onto the boardwalk and glared at Longarm in the light that came through the lobby windows. "You have no jurisdiction in Mexico, Señor Long."

"I know that," said Longarm, "but I still feel like it's my responsibility."

A new voice came from the doorway, but it was equally emphatic. "Absolutely not," said Franklin Barton as he moved out onto the boardwalk. "How can you even think of infringing on Mexico's sovereignty, Long, while these delicate negotiations are going on?"

"I'm thinking about a young woman who's probably mighty scared right now," Longarm snapped. He was in no mood to put up with Barton's pettiness.

"Please, Señor Long," Don Alfredo said slowly, almost painfully. "Señor Barton and Capitan Hernandez are correct. It would not be fitting for you to cross the border in pursuit of those outlaws, no matter who they may have as their prisoner. I know this as a diplomat and a representative of El Presidente." He cast a hard look at Barton and Hernandez, then gripped Longarm's arm again. "But as a father, I implore you, Señor Long . . . rescue my daughter. Bring her back safely to me."

"Out of the question," Barton said angrily, but the heavy clomp of booted footsteps made him fall silent.

Coffin strode up to the little group standing in front of the hotel. "Find that gal, Long?" he asked.

"I'm afraid not," Longarm told him.

"Well, I'm ready to ride with you when you go after them skunks. We'd best get a move on if we don't want 'em to have too big a lead."

Through clenched teeth, Barton said, "I was just trying to explain why you can't—"

Longarm ignored him and said to Guiterrez, "Are you sure this is what you want, Don Alfredo? You're liable to get in trouble with your own government if Coffin and I cross the border."

The Mexican diplomat shook his head. "I do not care. All that matters to me is Sonia's safety." He hesitated a moment, then added, "Besides, El Presidente owes me more than one favor. I can guarantee there will be no trouble from Diaz about this."

"That's good enough for me," said Longarm. He turned to Coffin. "Somebody's got to stay here—"

"Not me," Coffin cut in. "The doc's patchin' up Sanderson right now, and he says the sheriff's goin' to be good as new, 'cept for that busted wing. But it ain't his gun arm, so I reckon he can watch out over things here in town until reinforcements get here."

"Reinforcements?" repeated Longarm.

"I've done wired Austin already and got a reply back from Major Jones. He rousted out Cap'n McDowell, and ol' Roarin' Bill's sendin' Hatfield over here with a troop of

Rangers. They'll be here in less'n two days.'' Coffin pushed back the sombrero on his rumpled thatch of dark hair. ''But I reckon by that time, you and me'll be a good ways south of the Rio Grande, Long.''

Longarm nodded. ''Sounds good to me.'' He knew that the other Rangers would be more than capable of keeping the peace in Del Rio and protecting the diplomats while he and Coffin were gone.

''I'll get my hoss,'' Coffin said. ''That looks like a pretty good piece of horseflesh at the hitch rack, so you might want to hang on to it.''

Longarm thought the same thing. He was satisfied with the bay. He wanted to get his own saddle, his Winchester, and some supplies before he and Coffin set out into Mexico, though.

He got busy with those preparations while Franklin Barton and Capitan Hernandez followed him around, still complaining. The young American army officer, Jeffery Spooner, joined in and added his own voice to the chorus telling Longarm he couldn't go across the border. Finally, Don Alfredo was forced to say coldly, ''If you want these negotiations to continue, Señor Barton, you will allow Señor Long to go about his business without bothering him. And as for you, Capitan . . .'' Guiterrez launched into a spate of harsh, rapid Spanish, and the tongue-lashing caused Hernandez to jerk his head up and down in a curt, reluctant nod. Barton just shook his head and went off toward his suite, muttering under his breath.

Less than fifteen minutes had passed by the time Longarm and Coffin were mounted up in front of the hotel, ready to ride. Haggard, his face still drawn from shock and worry, Don Alfredo shook hands with both of them.

''*Vaya con Dios*,'' he said. ''Bring my daughter back to me, my friends.''

''You got our word on that,'' Coffin swore. Longarm just nodded and didn't say anything.

He hated to make promises he wasn't sure he could keep.

• • •

The moon was high in the sky, a great Cyclopean eye gazing down on the Rio Grande as the two riders crossed the border river a little later. Side by side, they moved up onto the southern bank and started across the flat, semi-arid plain. Within a matter of moments, they were out of sight of the river.

That was why neither Longarm nor Lazarus Coffin saw the man who crossed the river behind them a few minutes later. He was a tall figure in the moonlight, wearing a broad-brimmed black hat and riding a black stallion. As the horse's hooves splashed quietly in the waters of the Rio Grande, the man leaned forward slightly in the saddle, patted the magnificent animal on the shoulder, and said, "Well, here we go again, Phantom. Reckon one of these days, our luck's going to run out. I just hope it's not any time soon."

Chapter 10

Any hopes that Longarm and Coffin had harbored of catching up quickly to El Aguila's gang had faded by morning. The rising of the sun found them many miles deep into Mexico. Lack of sleep had made both men bone weary, and when Longarm suggested they call a short halt, Coffin made no objection.

"Leastways they ain't tryin' to hide their trail," said Coffin as he lowered his canteen from his mouth. He gestured at the tracks they were following, which were plainly visible in the reddish glare of the rising sun.

"I guess they figure they're not in much danger over here on this side of the border," Longarm replied. He pulled the cork from his own canteen, lifted it to his mouth, and took a short sip of the tepid liquid inside. While this part of the country wasn't exactly a desert, water holes weren't very common either. A man who wasted water around here might pay a very high price for such foolishness.

Horses had to drink too, so Longarm and Coffin dismounted and used their hats to water their mounts. Both Longarm's bay and Coffin's steel-dust gelding stuck their muzzles in the headgear and appreciatively sucked up the liquid.

"El Aguila and his men probably aren't very afraid of the *rurales*," Longarm went on, picking up the thread of their earlier comments, "and they know you and me ain't supposed to be over here chasing after them."

Coffin snorted in contempt. "I wouldn't be scared of *rurales* neither. That bunch is the sorriest excuse for lawmen—"

"They're not all bad," Longarm pointed out. "It's just that a lot of their officers are corrupt, and they're spread way too thin. True, most of 'em don't really give a damn, but some of them try to do their job."

Coffin looked like he would just as soon believe that a fella could flap his arms and fly to the moon. He took up the reins of the steel-dust and started walking so that the horse could rest. Longarm followed suit with the bay mare.

After a few minutes, Coffin said, "I done told you how come I'm wearin' this badge, Long. How'd you come to be a lawman?"

"It's something I sort of just drifted into," Longarm replied. That wasn't completely the truth, but it would do. "I came out West after the war and did some cowboying for a while, then figured out that was a good way to wind up old, stove up, and broke."

A grin spread across Coffin's bearded face. "So you took up a nice, safe, high-payin' job like manhuntin'."

"Yep, and wound up breaking a few bones and wearing out a few saddles anyway. But I'm pretty good at it, if I do say so myself. I've lived this long anyway."

"I had no notion I'd ever be a lawman. Hell, if anything, I figured I'd be ridin' the other side of the trail." Coffin shrugged his massive shoulders. "But I'm wearin' the badge now, and I plan to be the best Ranger I can be. I've met a bunch of 'em since I joined up, and they're good men."

Longarm thought about Billy Vail and nodded. "Yeah, they are . . . most of 'em."

Coffin let that pass. The two men walked on in silence for a few minutes. Then he asked, "You get any lovin' from Señorita Guiterrez?"

The bluntness of the question made Longarm frown in

surprise. He slid a cheroot from his vest pocket and put it in his mouth, then clenched it unlit between his teeth and said, "A gentleman don't talk about such things, old son."

Coffin laughed. "I didn't figure you'd got in her pants. She's the type that just likes to lead a fella on, get him all hot and bothered, then cut the legs out from under him." He shook his head. "She gave me all sorts of looks and even said some pretty bold things to me, but when it came time for her to actually do somethin' about it, she didn't want no part of it. No, sir, then she was just an *innocente* again."

Longarm chewed on the cheroot and didn't say anything. Coffin seemed as much amused as he was bothered by Sonia's teasing behavior, but Longarm figured that the Ranger probably wouldn't want to hear about what had been going on in that alley just before El Aguila's bunch had raided Del Rio again.

Instead of commenting, Longarm looked around, studying their surroundings. They were still traveling through flat land, but ranges of hills had risen to the east and west of them and appeared to gradually be drawing closer together. There were probably plenty of good hiding places in those hills, but the tracks of El Aguila's gang didn't veer off from their continued southerly direction.

Suddenly, as Longarm looked at the hills to the west, movement caught his eye. He turned his head so that he could look directly at the rocky upthrusts, and after a moment he asked casually, "You don't happen to have a pair of field glasses in those saddlebags of yours, do you, Coffin?"

"Nope. What is it you want to look at?"

Without stopping, Longarm nodded toward the hills he had been watching. "Take a look over yonder in those hills. See anything?"

For a long moment, Coffin didn't say anything as he squinted toward the distant heights. Then he growled, "Son of a bitch. Are those Yaquis?"

"That'd be my guess. I think I caught a flash of color a time or two from those bandannas they wear tied around their heads."

"Son of a bitch," Coffin said again. "We best make a

run for it.'' He turned toward his horse, ready to mount up.

''Hold on,'' Longarm said quickly. ''They're still a ways off, and they're just riding along through the hills, heading south like we are. Maybe they're not even interested in us.''

''You ever dealt with Yaquis before?''

''As a matter of fact, I have,'' said Longarm.

''Then you know it ain't smart to fool around with 'em. They like killin' better'n just about anything, and they like killin' white men best of all. I heard stories about how they caught a party of prospectors who'd come over here and tortured all of 'em to death.''

Longarm had heard similar stories, and knew that they had a basis in fact. The Yaquis, native to northern Mexico, were a fierce breed of people, and the Mexican government and military had had as much trouble with them over the years as the Americans had had with the Apaches and Comanches. Maybe even more, because as far as Longarm knew, none of the Yaquis were on reservations. They were all still living free in the mountains and foothills.

''Go ahead and mount up,'' Longarm told Coffin. ''If they've been watching us, they'll know that we were just resting the horses. So it won't be anything unusual if we start riding again.''

''You don't want 'em to know that we've seen 'em,'' said Coffin.

''That's the idea.'' Longarm pointed into the distance ahead of them. ''I think those two ranges run together somewhere up yonder, and if they do, there might be a place there we could fort up if need be.''

Coffin nodded grimly. ''Good idea. Them Yaquis come after us, they'll think they've grabbed aholt of a two-headed rattlesnake.'' He sounded almost as if he hoped that would come about.

Longarm certainly didn't share that opinion. He wasn't confident that he and Coffin could fight off an attack by the Indians, and if they were killed, that would leave no one to rescue Sonia Guiterrez from El Aguila.

Of course, Sonia might be dead already, he reminded himself bluntly. But they hadn't found her body anywhere along the trail, nor any fresh graves—as if outlaws like the ones they were pursuing would take the time to bury one of their victims—so Longarm was inclined to think that Sonia was still alive. A little the worse for wear maybe, but alive nonetheless.

He and Coffin swung up into their saddles and put the horses into a trot. There was a part of Longarm that wanted to urge the bay into a gallop, a mad dash for some hoped-for place of safety, but he suppressed that impulse. Better to take it slow and easy and see what happened.

Less than a half hour later, what happened was that the Yaquis rode down out of the hills and started angling toward them.

"Shoot!" exclaimed Coffin. "They're comin', Long."

"I see them," said Longarm. "Remember earlier, Coffin, when you were wanting to ride like hell?"

"Yeah?"

"Do it *now*!"

Longarm jabbed his heels into the bay's flanks and sent the mare leaping forward. There was no longer any point in trying to make the Yaquis think they hadn't been spotted. If Longarm and Coffin had any hope for survival, it lay in the speed of their horses—and pure luck.

Both men leaned over the necks of their mounts and urged them on. Longarm kept a close eye on the ground in front of him, watching for anything that might cause a misstep or a stumble by the mare. A fall would be disastrous right now. But he was unable to keep from glancing to the west, where the Yaquis were also riding hard now, trying to intercept the two lawmen. The Indian ponies, bred for riding in the mountains, were surefooted, but they were also short-legged and not overly blessed with speed. That was another cause for hope. A slim hope, to be sure, but any was better than none.

Gradually, Longarm's horse drew ahead of Coffin's. Neither man was a lightweight, but Coffin was bigger and heavier. Longarm glanced back, and saw the grim expression on the Ranger's face.

If it came down to brass tacks, Longarm wondered, would he leave Coffin behind? Even if only one of them survived,

Sonia Guiterrez would still have a chance. But could Longarm abandon a fellow lawman?

He hoped like hell he wouldn't have to make that choice.

A glance to the right and left showed him that the hills were definitely closer on both sides now. He had no idea what the terrain would be like where the two ranges came together. The hills might even form a box canyon, in which case Longarm and Coffin were riding into a trap from which there would be no escape. But out here on the flat there was no place that could be defended from the Yaquis, so they didn't really have anywhere else to go.

Longarm saw a dark line on the horizon ahead of him. That had to be where the hills joined, he thought. But it was still a couple of miles away, and the Yaquis were only a few hundred yards off to the right and closing quickly.

"Run, damn it, run!" Coffin bellowed at the steel-dust as he lashed at the horse with the reins. The steel-dust responded, drawing almost even with Longarm's bay once more.

Longarm checked the position of the Yaquis, then shouted over the thunder of the hoofbeats, "They can't cut us off! They're going to have to run us down from behind!"

"I can see the hills!" Coffin called back, lifting an arm to point. Longarm just nodded and didn't waste any more breath on talk.

Those two miles seemed to take forever to cover. As Longarm had predicted, he and Coffin swept out ahead of the Yaquis, who fell in behind them. Longarm thought he heard the distant cracking of rifles, but he didn't look back. It was almost impossible to hit anything by shooting from the back of a running horse. If one of the bullets fired by the Yaquis found him or Coffin, then the hand of Fate would be guiding it, and there was no use arguing with Fate.

None of the bullets came close enough for the two lawmen to hear their passage through the air. Longarm kept his gaze fastened on the line of hills in front of them, which he could plainly see now. As they drew closer still, he began to be able to make out a cluster of boulders scattered along the line where the hills rose from the plain. Longarm's heart thudded a little more heavily. He and Coffin could fort up in those rocks and hold off the Yaquis until their ammunition ran out. With any luck, the Indians would give up before then.

"Head for those rocks!" Coffin shouted unnecessarily at him. Longarm was already riding as hard as he could toward the boulders.

He looked back again. The Yaquis were still a couple of hundred yards behind. The stubby ponies hadn't been able to close the gap any more than that.

"Come on, come on," Longarm said under his breath to the bay, and the mare gave it her all. Hooves thudding against the hard ground, she ran between two of the big rocks, followed closely by the steel-dust carrying Coffin.

Longarm reined in, bringing the bay to a sliding halt. He was out of the saddle instantly, pulling the Winchester from its saddle boot with him. A few yards away, Coffin was flinging himself off the steel-dust, and his Winchester was in his hands too. Without taking the time to tie the horses to any of the scrubby brush that grew between the boulders, Longarm and Coffin crouched behind the rocks and leveled their rifles at the Yaquis. Both Winchesters cracked almost simultaneously.

A couple of the Indians went spinning off the colorful blankets they used instead of saddles. As the echoes of the shots died away, Longarm heard outraged cries from the other Yaquis. The war party abruptly split up, some of the riders veering to the right, some to the left, and the rest coming straight on.

"Damn and blast," muttered Coffin. "Somebody's been teachin' those redskins army tactics."

"They knew 'em before the army ever did," said Longarm as he levered another shell into the firing chamber of the Winchester. "The Comanches were the best light cavalrymen that ever sat a horse, and these Yaquis ain't bad either, though they do most of their fighting on foot whenever they can. Best get ready on your side, Coffin, they're going to try to flank us!"

"I know it, I know it," Coffin said as he turned to his left to cover the slopes of the hills in that direction. ''But what about those ol' boys in the middle?''

That was the problem, all right, Longarm thought. Maybe he and Coffin could prevent any of the Yaquis from getting behind them—maybe. But if they did that, they would be overrun by the ones coming straight toward them. On the other hand, if they concentrated their fire on the Yaquis charging straight ahead, the flanking parties would sweep around them and catch them in a deadly cross fire. Two men couldn't fight off an attack coming from three directions—it was as simple as that.

If they'd only had a third man . . .

''Who the hell's *that*?''

Longarm glanced at Coffin, and saw that the Ranger was staring back in the direction they had come from. Longarm looked that way too, and as he did, he heard the crackle of gunfire. Peering past the attacking Yaquis, Longarm suddenly spotted a tall figure on a black horse. The stranger was racing up behind the Yaquis, taking them by surprise, and guiding his mount with his knees as he filled his hands with a pair of revolvers and opened fire. Lead slashed into the Yaquis from this unexpected direction, dropping several of them and making the others cry out in rage and frustration.

''Somebody's giving us a hand!'' Longarm called to Coffin. ''Let's don't waste it! Watch out on your side!''

Longarm threw his rifle to his shoulder and began blazing away at the Yaquis trying to skirt the rocks to the right. He fired as fast as he could work the Winchester's lever, and was rewarded by the sight, glimpsed through a haze of powder smoke, of several Indians tumbling lifelessly from their ponies. The others hauled their mounts around, turned back by the withering hail of lead thrown out by Longarm.

On the other side of the cluster of boulders, Coffin was doing likewise. His shots weren't quite as accurate as Longarm's, but he dropped enough of the Yaquis to force them to retreat. The flanking maneuver had failed, and the stranger on the black horse was still wreaking havoc among the rest of the war party.

Suddenly, all the surviving Yaquis broke and ran, riding

hard toward the hills to the west, which were more rugged than those to the east or south. The riderless ponies followed them. Longarm and Coffin stood up in order to throw some final shots after them, and the stranger holstered his smoking Colts and drew his own Winchester from its sheath. He added his fire to that of Longarm and Coffin. The raking shots followed the Yaquis and kept them moving until they had disappeared over a distant crest.

Coffin turned to Longarm. "Think they'll be back?"

"I don't know, but I plan to reload as quick as I can anyway," replied Longarm. He went over to the bay, which was waiting close by with reins trailing on the rocky ground, and took a box of cartridges from the saddlebags. He thumbed fresh ones into the loading gate of the rifle, and then picked up the empty brass that had scattered around his feet as he ejected the spent shells.

"Here comes that fella," said Coffin. Longarm looked up and saw the stranger jogging easily toward them on the big black horse.

Only he wasn't completely a stranger, Longarm realized with a surge of recognition. He had seen this man before.

"Howdy, fellas," the rider said in a deep, resonant voice as he brought the black to a halt at the edge of the rocks. "Looked like you had a mess of trouble on your plates. Hope you don't mind that I helped clean it up."

"I don't mind one damn bit, mister," Coffin said fervently. "As far as I can see, you saved our bacon just now, and I'm mighty obliged."

"Glad to help." The man cuffed back his broad-brimmed hat, and the smile that played across his wide mouth relieved the grim cast of his features with their hawklike nose, strong jaw, and cold eyes of pale gray. "Name's Walt Scott."

"I'm Lazarus Coffin, and this here's Custis Long." Coffin grinned. "What're the odds we'd run into another gringo this far south of the border right when we needed help?"

Longarm wondered that too, and wondered as well just how much of a coincidence it was that this stranger who called himself Walt Scott had shown up at just the right moment to help them.

Because the last time Longarm had seen him, Scott had been in Kilroy's Saloon in Del Rio several days earlier. He had even exchanged a few words with the man before Scott left the saloon. What was it the bartender had said about him? That he had the look of a gunfighting drifter, Longarm recalled.

That was sure enough true. And now here he was, coming to the rescue of Longarm and Coffin. It was enough to make a man curious. . . .

But Scott *had* saved their bacon, just as Coffin had said, so it was only right that they share it with him.

"Light and sit," Longarm told the stranger. "Had breakfast yet?"

"Can't say as I have," replied Scott. "In fact, my provisions are a mite low. But I do have some Arbuckle's we can cook up."

"Sounds good to me," said Coffin. He rubbed his bearded jaw and frowned in thought. "Might even have a proposition for you, Scott."

Longarm knew what Coffin meant by that comment. Three men would stand a better chance of freeing Sonia Guiterrez from El Aguila, especially when the third man was such a ring-tailed heller as Walt Scott seemed to be.

Scott swung down from the black stallion with a grin. "I'm always interested," he said, "as long as the proposition's a paying one."

I'll just bet you are, old son, thought Longarm. *I'll just bet you are.*

Chapter 11

Under the circumstances, Longarm and Coffin couldn't pause long for breakfast, but it didn't take much time to build a small, almost smokeless fire to brew some coffee and fry a few strips of bacon for each of the three men. They also chewed on some biscuits Coffin had brought along from Del Rio.

"What brings you gents down here?" asked Walt Scott as he hunkered on his heels next to the fire.

"Might ask you the same thing," said Longarm, "seeing as how you're a *norte americano* like we are. And you were in Del Rio a few days ago, just like us."

Scott's eyes narrowed as he looked at Longarm. "Say, you do look familiar. We ran into each other in Kilroy's place, didn't we?"

Longarm didn't believe for a second that Scott had forgotten about their previous meeting until now. But if that was the way the man wanted to play it for the time being, Longarm was willing to go along with him. The marshal was a firm believer in the old saying about giving a man enough rope to hang himself.

"That's right," Longarm said with a nod. "You were drinking beer, I ordered Maryland rye."

Scott returned the nod. "Yep, I recall now."

"You fellas can discuss your drinkin' habits another time," Coffin put in. "Right now we got more important things to talk about. Scott, me and Long are lawmen, and we're down here south of the border chasin' a no-account bastard name of El Aguila. Ever heard of him?"

"The name's vaguely familiar," said Scott. "How come a couple of American badge-toters are operating in Mexico?"

Longarm might have preferred feeling Scott out a little more before bluntly admitting their identities like that, but Coffin didn't have much subtlety about him. Anyway, there wasn't really time to be subtle, Longarm reminded himself.

"We're here at the express invitation of a representative of the Mexican government," Longarm said. "El Aguila and his men raided Del Rio last night, and they kidnapped a Mexican citizen. A young woman."

Scott nodded. "So that's who left those tracks I spotted earlier. The outlaws are headed south, I reckon?"

Coffin said, "They must have a hideout down here. But Long and me figure on rootin' 'em out and gettin' that gal back. How 'bout joinin' up with us?"

Scott sipped his coffee from a tin cup. "You believe in plain talk, don't you, Lazarus?"

"Every day that passes is a step closer to the grave," replied the big Ranger. "Man who don't say what he means and don't ask for what he wants is a damn fool."

"Could be you're right," allowed Scott. He didn't answer Coffin's question, though.

"Well, what's it goin' to be?" demanded Coffin after a moment. "Are you with us or not?"

"Maybe Scott's got something else he has to do, or someplace else he has to be," Longarm said, watching Scott's reaction—or lack of one.

Scott shook his head. "Nope, I'm just drifting. I'd just as soon be one place as another, and hunting down some outlaws with you boys sounds like it might be plumb entertaining." He tossed the dregs of his coffee into the fire. "Sure, I'll throw in with you. Thanks for the invitation."

Coffin finished his own coffee and stood up. "We better get movin', then. I figure El Aguila ain't hurryin' too much, since he don't know we're back here followin' him, but we don't want him gettin' too far ahead of us."

"The outlaws could have heard those shots," Scott pointed out as the three men got ready to ride again. "Sound travels a long way out here."

"But they won't know who was doing the shooting," said Longarm. "You're right, though. We'd better not waste any more time."

Within a matter of minutes, they were mounted up and had found the tracks of El Aguila's gang. The outlaws had continued south, riding up into the hills. The ground was harder and dotted with stretches of rock, which made following the tracks more difficult, but all three of the pursuers had keen eyesight. If one of them lost the trail momentarily, another soon picked it up.

Longarm expected Scott to ask more questions about the captive they were trying to rescue, but the tall drifter didn't seem particularly curious about Sonia. It was possible, thought Longarm, that everything Scott had told them was true. Some men were just too fiddle-footed to stay in one place for very long, and such types generally didn't pay too much attention to things like borders. Riding across Mexico was just as good as riding across Texas to men like that. And the excitement of a good fight with an owlhoot gang, despite its dangers, could be a powerful lure to such an individual.

But every instinct Longarm possessed told him there was more to Scott than met the eye. He resolved to keep a close watch on the man. If Scott was telling the truth, he would likely be a valuable ally. If not, he might turn out to be more dangerous than El Aguila himself.

Midday came and went, and the sun blazed down on the three men, forcing them to stop fairly often and rest the horses. They tried to find some shade whenever they paused, and were usually able to do so. As they climbed higher into the hills, there was more vegetation, including mesquite and cedar trees.

At one such halt, Scott poured water into his hat for his horse and said, "Here you go, Phantom."

Coffin frowned. "You gave your horse a name?"

"Why not?"

"I never heard of nobody namin' their horse. Hell, you might as well give your gun a name."

"What about Old Betsy, Davy Crockett's long rifle?" Scott asked. "Davy was fond of that flintlock, and I'm fond of Phantom here. We've ridden many a trail together, and he's saved my life more than once."

Longarm was lounging in the shade of a cedar tree. He spoke up, saying, "I've ridden some good horses, but I don't recall ever naming one. Of course, they've usually been rented or borrowed mounts, so I didn't have them for very long."

"Just strikes me as foolishness, that's all," said Coffin. "Seems like it'd be harder to ride an animal into the ground if you had to if it had a name you'd given to it."

Scott shrugged. "You're something of a philosopher, Lazarus, but on matters of philosophy, men often have to agree to disagree."

"Huh? Oh. Yeah, I reckon you're right. But I still wouldn't give a hoss a name."

Longarm just chuckled and shook his head. He would remember in the future to leave the arguing with Coffin to Walt Scott.

If there was a future after they caught up with El Aguila's gang . . .

By late afternoon, they hadn't caught up with the outlaws, but Longarm was convinced the tracks they were following were fresher. He estimated they were only a couple of hours behind now. But even with the frequent rests, the horses were getting tired, and so were Longarm and Coffin. Neither man had gotten any sleep the night before, and dozing for a minute or two in the saddle every now and then didn't do much to refresh a man. Longarm's eyeballs were beginning to feel like they had been plucked out, rolled around in sand for a while, then stuck back in their sockets. He was rubbing them when Coffin said, "Well, looky there."

Longarm looked, and saw that the Ranger was pointing at the tracks they had been following. The trail split, one group of tracks vanishing through a narrow gap between some hills, the other winding down a ridge toward a broad, shallow valley.

"There's a village down there," said Scott, nodding toward the valley.

Longarm saw the settlement too. It was a small cluster of adobe buildings, the largest of them crowned by a square bell tower. That would be the local mission. The other structures were probably a cantina or two, maybe a store, and the homes of the farmers who worked the land alongside a narrow creek that ran through the valley.

Coffin looked at him. "That bunch we've been followin' split up, Long. What do we do now?"

Longarm frowned in thought. Which group of outlaws would have been the most likely to take Sonia with them, the ones that had headed for the village or the bunch riding on further into the hills? He couldn't answer that question, because there was no way of knowing what the men intended to do with their captive. Longarm had figured they would all head for El Aguila's hideout, but it was possible they had taken Sonia down to the settlement, planning to sell her to the owner of the cantina as a whore. Or maybe they had something else entirely in mind.

"We could split up," Scott suggested.

Longarm shook his head. "There's not enough of us. One man would have to ride alone."

"Wouldn't be the first time I've done that," Scott said quietly.

"No, we'll stay together." Longarm was emphatic about that. He reached another decision and went on. "We'll ride on down to that village. It won't take long, and if the girl's not there, we can always pick up the trail again here."

"What if we find some of those outlaws but not the gal?" asked Coffin.

"Then they can tell us where the others are taking her, can't they?" Longarm said with a tired grin.

"I'm sure they'll be glad to cooperate," Scott added dryly.

Coffin reined his horse around. "All right, all right, let's just get on with it."

The three of them rode openly down the trail that led to the Mexican village. It was past siesta time, and as they approached, Longarm saw several *peones* in sombreros, white shirts and trousers, and rope-soled sandals moving around the adobe buildings. One of the buildings had half-a-dozen horses tied up at a hitch rail in front of it, marking it as the cantina, even though there was no sign painted on it. The door was open, and the arched entranceway reminded Longarm of the mouth of a cave. With the glare of the lowering sun flooding the dusty street, it was impossible to see anything in the shadowy interior of the cantina. The skin on the back of Longarm's neck prickled as he rode closer to the building.

"Careful, boys, careful," breathed Coffin, who was evidently feeling some of the same sensations. Even the easygoing Scott seemed more tense than usual.

But no shots came from inside the cantina, and the men Longarm, Coffin, and Scott passed on the street looked at them with only the casual interest they would direct toward any strangers.

There was room at the hitch rack for the three horses, but that just about filled it up. Longarm looped the bay's reins around the rail, tying them loosely so that they could be jerked free in a hurry if need be. Coffin and Scott followed suit.

"I'll go in first," Longarm said quietly. "You two hang back a little, in case there's trouble right away."

Coffin looked as if he wanted to argue, but Scott nodded and said, "All right." Coffin shrugged and waited with Scott as Longarm walked over to the door of the cantina.

The inside of the place was lit by several candles, Longarm saw as he stepped through the doorway. His eyes adjusted quickly to the dimness. Over the years, he had been in probably a hundred cantinas similar to this one. A crude bar ran across the back of the room, built of rough-hewn planks laid across the tops of several barrels. The floor was hard-packed dirt, and scattered around it were a handful of tables and chairs, all of them as crudely made as the bar. Another arched doorway, this one covered by a beaded curtain, led into a room in the back. A few Mexican farmers stood at the bar, being served by a grossly fat woman in a peasant blouse that revealed far too much of her pendulous breasts. A quick glance around told Longarm that the woman behind the bar was the only female in the place.

All the tables were unoccupied except for one in the corner. Six men were crowded around it, passing a bottle of tequila from hand to hand as they played cards and smoked small black cigars that looked like burning pieces of rope. Smelled like it too, thought Longarm as he moved unhurriedly toward the bar. As he reached it and turned slightly, he saw Coffin and Scott step through the door of the cantina.

In the brief moments since he had entered the building, several pieces of information had burned themselves into Longarm's brain. For one thing, he was convinced the men at the table were members of El Aguila's gang. Four of them were Mexicans, the other two gringos, but they were all cut from the same cloth—hardcases, each and every one. For another, they were drunk and not paying attention to anything except their celebrating. That meant the loot from the latest raid on Del Rio had probably been split up already.

Their inattention to the newcomers also meant that no one had warned them about the three men riding into the village. Evidently none of the townspeople felt any great liking for these members of El Aguila's gang. Still, Longarm was a little surprised that fear hadn't prompted someone to try to curry favor with the desperadoes by telling them about the strangers.

These folks really didn't like El Aguila, Longarm realized. That was all right with him.

The only real disappointment was the fact that Sonia wasn't there.

Or maybe she was. As Longarm rested his left hand on the bar, he heard an unmistakable sound—the moans and sighs of a woman caught up in the throes of passion. The noises were coming from the back room. Whoever was back there sounded as if she liked what was happening to her. Longarm's jaw tightened. He hated to think that maybe Sonia was *enjoying* her captivity.

The woman behind the bar edged over to him, a nervous expression on her face. "You want something?" she asked in heavily accented English.

"Tequila," said Longarm. He glanced over his shoulder. Coffin and Scott were staying close to the door, lounging with their shoulders against the adobe wall. The outlaws in the corner hadn't glanced toward them, as far as Longarm could tell.

The sounds of lovemaking had ended in the back room. With a clatter, the curtain of beads was shoved aside. Longarm turned his head and saw a young woman step out into the main room. The neckline of her blouse was pulled down so that half of one brown nipple was visible. She had a satisfied smile on her face.

But she wasn't Sonia Guiterrez.

The woman behind the bar thumped down a glass in front of Longarm and splashed some tequila in it from a bottle. As Longarm reached for it, a man followed the younger woman out of the back room. He was smirking, clearly pleased with himself.

But when his gaze locked with Longarm's, his eyes widened and his hand dropped in a blur to the gun on his hip.

A couple of thoughts whipped through Longarm's brain in that instant. He had figured that because there were six horses at the hitch rail outside and six men around the table in the corner, all of the outlaws were accounted for. But the man who had come out of the back room, the man who was now grabbing for his gun as a curse sprang to his lips, had definitely recognized Longarm. And Longarm thought he recognized the man too. He remembered the duster the man wore, and the cream-colored hat with conchos around the band.

The last time Longarm had seen him, he'd been tossing a stick of dynamite into Sheriff Sanderson's office in Del Rio.

All of that flashed through Longarm's mind even as he acted. He flicked his left wrist, and the tequila in the glass he held in that hand flew up into the face of the outlaw. At the same time Longarm twisted toward the man, his right hand flashing across his body to palm the Colt out of the cross-draw rig. The outlaw in the duster yelled in pain as the tequila stung his eyes. He stumbled back a step as he blinked furiously. His gun was already out, and it was coming up fast, even though he was half-blinded.

Longarm triggered twice, the slugs slamming into the outlaw's midsection at close range and driving him backward like a giant hammer. Before the man even hit the dirt of the floor, Longarm was spinning around toward the table where the other owlhoots were.

One of the men at the table went diving away from the others, indicating to Longarm that he was probably one of the locals and not a member of the gang at all. The others were all leaping to their feet and reaching for their guns.

"Hold it!" yelled Coffin, who had drawn the pearl-handled Remington. The long-barreled revolver was leveled at the outlaws.

They ignored the command, as Longarm expected they would. Everyone else in the cantina had wisely hit the floor, so Longarm and Coffin had a clear field as they opened fire. The gunshots were deafening as their thunder filled the low-ceilinged cantina.

From the corner of his eye, Longarm saw Scott tip over one of the tables and crouch behind it for cover. The drifter had drawn his guns, but he hadn't fired yet. Of course, he didn't really need to. Longarm and Coffin had had the drop on the outlaws, and it had been foolish of the men not to surrender. Most owlhoots weren't noted for the sharpness of their wits. These had tried to blaze away at Longarm and Coffin, and were getting cut down for their trouble.

The shooting lasted only a handful of seconds, though it seemed longer. A couple of the outlaws were thrown back against the adobe wall behind them by the lead plowing into their chests. Another doubled over, gutshot, and collapsed onto the table where they had been playing poker, scattering the cards. The pasteboards fluttered to the ground, stained with outlaw blood.

That left just two of the gang on their feet, and one of them was wounded. The man dropped his gun and clutched at a bullet-shattered elbow. He whimpered and cursed in pain as he stumbled against a chair. The other man let his gun fall to the floor too, though he wasn't wounded. He lifted his hands and cried out, "Don't shoot! For God's sake, don't shoot no more!"

The man who was surrendering was one of the gringos, Longarm saw. His companion with the broken arm was Mexican. The fight was out of both of them, and as Longarm and Coffin approached, guns still leveled, they cringed back.

As all the innocent bystanders in the cantina scurried out the front door of the place, including the barmaid, Longarm kicked the fallen guns out of reach and said harshly, "You're two of El Aguila's men. No use in denying it. We trailed you here from Del Rio."

The Mexican with the wounded arm spat at Longarm's feet. There were tears in his eyes and his face was contorted in pain, but he found the strength somewhere inside him to put up a stubbornly defiant front. "We deny nothing," he said.

Scott had followed Coffin. He checked the men on the floor and announced, "These boys are all dead. That was pretty good shooting."

Longarm grunted and bit back a comment about how that was no thanks to Scott's efforts. The man was no coward—he had proved that when he took on those Yaquis—but for some reason he had decided to remain in the background this time.

Longarm might have puzzled over that more, but right now he was more worried about Sonia Guiterrez. "Where's the girl you took from Del Rio?" he asked the two survivors.

The American started to say something, but the wounded Mexican cut him off. "You gringo lawmen will never find her," he gloated. "She has been taken to our stronghold, where not even an army of bastards like you could reach her."

"I wouldn't be so sure about that, old son," Longarm said.

"I would," said Walt Scott. The words were accompanied by the ominous double click of gun hammers being cocked.

And those sounds told Longarm just what a damn fool he had been.

Chapter 12

"You're double-crossing us, aren't you, Scott?" Longarm said.

"Afraid so. Drop your gun, Long. You too, Coffin."

Coffin started cursing, a venomous rant that fairly stank of brimstone. After a moment, Longarm interrupted him by saying, "That's not going to do any good, Coffin. Scott's got us where he wants us."

"Yes, and if you don't drop those guns, I'm going to have to shoot you," Scott warned. "I don't particularly want to—"

"Sure you don't, you sneakin', yella-bellied, goat-lovin' excuse for a human bein'!" said Coffin. "I'd like to get my hands around your throat just for a minute! I'd—"

Scott prodded Coffin in the back with the long barrel of his right-hand gun. Reluctantly, Coffin shut up and lowered his Remington to the floor. He dropped it carefully on the hard-packed dirt.

Longarm did likewise with his Colt, and Scott said in satisfaction, "That's better."

The wounded Mexican outlaw asked, "Why are you doing this, señor?"

"You mean Scott's not one of the gang?" The surprised question came from Longarm.

Scott chuckled coldly. "Not yet. But I'm going to be."

Understanding dawned in Longarm's brain. "You're going to turn us over to El Aguila. Buy your way into his bunch with a couple of gringo lawmen."

"Now you're thinking, Custis. I'm a man who likes to seize an opportunity when it presents itself. I don't reckon I'll ever get a better one."

The Mexican bandit turned to his uninjured companion. "Bind up this wound, Grady," he ordered, "and then get me a bottle of tequila. I am in great pain."

"Sure," Grady said with a nod. Now that the threat from Longarm and Coffin was over, he didn't look nearly as frightened. "Listen, Manuel, you know I didn't really mean to tell these law-dogs anything."

Manuel gave a skeptical snort, but made no other reply. Instead he glared at Longarm and said, "It was your bullet that shattered my arm, bastard. It will never be right again. I shall not forget."

Longarm didn't say anything in response to the implied threat, but Coffin spat on the floor and said with a scowl, "I hope you die of blood poisonin'."

Scott moved around so that he could cover Longarm and Coffin from the front. "Sit down at one of those tables, boys," he ordered. "It'll still be a while before we're ready to leave, I imagine." He glanced over at Manuel as the Mexican sat down at another table, moving somewhat awkwardly due to the way he clutched his wounded arm. "You *will* take me to see El Aguila, I assume."

"I have little choice but to take you to our stronghold," said Manuel. "Otherwise you might betray Grady and me just as you betrayed these men who thought you their friend."

"The odds *are* pretty much even now," Scott said with a grim smile playing across his wide mouth.

"That is why you did not declare yourself until the rest of my *compadres* were dead," Manuel said accusingly.

Scott shrugged broad shoulders. "Sometimes a man has to wait a bit to see which way he wants to jump. Anyway, the ball got rolling before I could do anything about it. Personally, I don't like to see a lot of killing."

Longarm managed not to laugh scornfully at that statement. He doubted that killing bothered Scott a bit. The self-proclaimed drifter was a cold-blooded son of a bitch, that was for sure.

And Longarm was kicking himself for not realizing what Scott had had in mind. He hadn't fully trusted Scott, not even after the man had pitched in to help fight off the Yaquis, but his concern for Sonia's whereabouts and well-being, along with the excitement of the gunfight with the outlaws, had made him let down his guard. If he got out of this mess alive, that wasn't going to happen again, he vowed.

Of course, it was looking mighty doubtful that he would have to worry about that. Once El Aguila got his hands on the two lawmen, they probably wouldn't live very long.

While Scott kept his guns trained on Longarm and Coffin, the barrels rock-steady in his firm grip, Grady patched up Manuel's arm as best he could. Manuel slugged down half a bottle of tequila to dull the pain from the injury, then got unsteadily to his feet. "Come," he said. "We ride for the hills."

Scott gestured with the twin Colts, motioning Longarm and Coffin onto their feet. Supported by Grady, Manuel stumbled out of the cantina, followed by Longarm and Coffin with Scott bringing up the rear. "What about the bodies of your friends?" Scott asked.

Manuel's right arm was supported in a crude sling that Grady had rigged. He waved his left arm without looking around. "Leave them," he said with the typical callousness of the outlaw breed. "They are no longer any use to us."

The sun had set behind the hills to the west, leaving the shadows of dusk gathering in the little village. Nervous faces watched from the windows of the other buildings as Longarm and Coffin were forced at gunpoint to mount up. Grady helped Manuel onto his horse, then kept a pistol trained on Longarm and Coffin while Scott swung up into the saddle atop Phantom. Once Grady was mounted too, he gathered up the reins of the horses belonging to the dead men inside the cantina and led them as the little group started up the slope to the point in the ridge where the trail had split.

Longarm took a deep breath and suppressed the anger he felt inside. He had to think clearly and calmly now; his life, as well as those of Coffin and Sonia, might depend on it.

There *was* one good thing about this, he reminded himself. He and Coffin were being taken straight to the gang's hide-out. That was something they might not have been able to accomplish without being captured. Now all they would have to do was escape from their captors, free Sonia, and take her with them when they fled.

Yep, thought Longarm grimly, that was all. . . .

Despite the pain of his wound and the fact that he was half drunk, Manuel was able to lead the group along a trail that wound like a maze through the hills. Longarm had figured out by now that Grady was a half-wit, at best, relying on the Mexican to tell him what to do.

Coffin was still muttering sulphurous curses under his breath as he rode alongside Longarm. Their hands were not tied, and Longarm hoped that fact wouldn't give Coffin the false confidence to try some sort of escape. Scott rode right behind them, and Longarm had seen the man's speed and accuracy with those black-handled Colts he wore. If Coffin made a break for it, Scott could shoot him down with little or no trouble. A dead lawman might be just as good to El Aguila as a live one.

Stars glittered brightly overhead in the vast sable cloak of night. As usual in this part of the world, the temperature cooled off rapidly once the sun was down, and by the time the group had been riding for a couple of hours after leaving the village, Longarm wished he could get his coat out of his saddlebags. The air had a definite chill in it.

Or maybe it was just the knowledge that he was being taken into the stronghold of a bloodthirsty outlaw gang at gunpoint that made icy fingers play along his spine, he thought. It wasn't the first time he had been in a spot this tight, but knowing that didn't help overmuch.

The landscape had grown even more rugged. Some of the hills were small mountains now. The trail wound between them. Longarm tried to keep track of landmarks so that he could find his way back along this path if he got the opportunity, but the darkness made that difficult. Manuel must have a good sense of direction, Longarm mused, or they would have been hopelessly lost by now.

Maybe they were, he thought. Maybe that was exactly what had happened. Manuel might not be thinking or seeing as clearly as he believed he was, and they might be wandering around aimlessly. Longarm hoped that wasn't the case. The one ray of light in this seemingly hopeless situation was the prospect that he and Coffin were being taken to the same place where Sonia was held prisoner.

As those thoughts were going through Longarm's head, the trail rounded a bend and ran through a narrow gap between two huge upthrusts of rock. Beyond this natural gateway, Longarm saw, moonlight washed down over a good-sized valley with overhanging cliffs on both sides that came together at the far end to form a blank wall. The valley looked as if it could have been formed by a giant hand molding mountains out of clay, then pressing a thumb down in the center of them. The gap seemed to be the only entrance.

And a few men could hold that gap against an army for a good while, decided Longarm. That was what made this such a good hideout. Lights glittered on the floor of the valley, and he knew there must be buildings down there.

A harsh voice hailed the party. "Who's there?" Longarm couldn't see the sentry, but he was willing to bet that more than one rifle was trained on them at this moment, and if the wrong answer came back, a hail of lead would fall on them.

"It is Manuel," called the wounded outlaw. "I am hurt, *muchachos*. Grady is with me, but the others are dead."

"Who're those other three bastards, then?" asked the hidden guard.

"Two of them are gringo lawmen from Texas," replied Manuel. "The other is a man who wishes to become one of us. He kept the lawmen from capturing Grady and me after they had killed the rest of our *compadres*."

Longarm wanted to point out that he wasn't from Texas at all, but had been born and bred in West-by-God Virginia, but he supposed that didn't really matter much right now. He kept his mouth shut.

"This ain't some sort of trick, is it?" the sentry asked suspiciously.

"You have my word it is not," answered Manuel, his voice thick and a little slurred. "Now, we must pass. My arm is hurting a great deal, and I would have the *curandero* attend to it."

So the outlaws had a physician among them, a former doctor maybe, or at least somebody with some medical training who had wound up following the owlhoot trail instead of the healer's road. That came as no surprise. Bandits got shot up all the time, and they would need someone to take care of their wounds.

"Go ahead," said the guard. "I reckon it's all right. Deke ain't goin' to be happy about those other boys gettin' themselves killed. He didn't want y'all goin' off to get drunk and play cards in the first place."

"Deke is not . . . the boss," said Manuel, the words coming now between teeth clenched in pain. That tequila was starting to wear off, Longarm figured.

"Maybe not, but he thinks he's in charge," said the hidden sentry.

Manuel heeled his horse into motion, riding through the gap trailed by Grady. The opening was so narrow that Longarm and Coffin had to go through it single file. Scott brought up the rear, as he had ever since they'd left the village.

The trail sloped down to the valley floor at a fairly sharp angle. Once they reached the bottom, Longarm saw in the moonlight that there was lush grass on the ground, along with clumps of trees here and there. This bowl in the mountains would have made a nice ranch, and perhaps that was what it had been at one time. As they neared the lights, Longarm saw that the yellow glow came from the windows of a large adobe house built in the Spanish style. The hacienda of the valley's former owner? That was likely, thought Longarm. But had the rancher abandoned the place for some reason, or been killed when El Aguila's gang took it over? Longarm couldn't answer that one.

They were challenged again as they approached an adobe wall that surrounded the hacienda. Double gates of black wrought iron were closed, blocking off the courtyard inside the wall. Manuel identified himself again, and shadowy figures carrying rifles appeared inside the gates and opened them.

"If I was you, *mi amigo,*" one of the men said to Manuel, "I would speak to Deke first before seeking out the *curandero*. Those empty saddles will not please him."

"The fault was not mine," protested Manuel. "But you are probably right."

Scott spoke up for the first time in quite a while. "I want to see this fella Deke myself. Sounds like he's the second in command around here, and I'll probably have to go through him to get to El Aquila."

Manuel laughed humorlessly. "*Sí*. This is true. Come with me."

He rode through the gates and into the courtyard, followed by the others. Coffin muttered, "Damn," as the gates clanged shut behind them. Longarm guessed the Ranger didn't care for the sound. From what he knew of Coffin's past, the big man had heard such sounds plenty of times before, as jail cells were closed and locked with Coffin on the wrong side of the bars.

Even in the shadows, the house was an impressive U-shaped structure with two stories, the second one with a balcony running along its entire length. A wrought-iron railing bordered the balcony. Lamplight came from several of the windows on both floors. Somewhere, someone was playing a guitar, and a faint hint of wood smoke filled the air along with the melodic notes. Under other circumstances, this would have been a peaceful, beautiful place.

For Longarm and Coffin, it was more than likely a death trap.

Manuel reined in at a hitch rack bordering the stone-paved patio between the wings of the house. He gave Grady a curt command to help him down. Grady did so, then turned and covered Longarm and Coffin while Scott dismounted. The routine was the reverse of what they had gone through when they left the isolated village.

A few moments later, Longarm and Coffin had dismounted as well, and Scott said dryly, "After you, boys."

Coffin growled a few more curses as he followed Manuel and Grady across the patio and through an open door into a large low-ceilinged room. Longarm was beside him, eyes flicking quickly around the room, taking in the scene and judging the odds.

No one else was in the room at the moment. It was furnished with heavy divans and chairs, and a thickly woven Indian rug lay on the stone floor. On one side of the room was a huge fireplace. It was a simple, yet comfortable room, no doubt reflecting the tastes of the original owner. Once again Longarm wondered what had become of him.

A door on the far side of the room opened, and a tall rawboned man in denim pants and a gray shirt walked in. There was something familiar about him, and after a second Longarm realized where he had seen the man before. This hombre was the one he had pegged as possibly being El Aguila during the first raid on Del Rio. The man had ridden in the forefront of the raiders galloping up and down the street.

Now, like all the other outlaws, he was unmasked, and Longarm saw an ugly, lantern-jawed face topped by thinning fair hair. He scowled at the newcomers and said, "I hear there was trouble, Manuel. What happened?"

Manuel half-turned toward Longarm and Coffin and indicated them with a curt wave of his uninjured arm. "These two men attacked us in the cantina. Higgins must have recognized one or both of them from Del Rio, because he went for his gun first. That one killed him." Manuel nodded toward Longarm. "The *bastardo* broke my arm with a bullet too. They killed everyone except for Grady and myself."

"It was a close one, Deke," put in Grady, clearly eager to mollify the lantern-jawed man. "They never would have got any of us if they hadn't taken us by surprise."

"They wouldn't have taken you by surprise if you weren't

idiots,'' said Deke with a disdainful curl of his upper lip. ''None of you could wait to take your share of the loot and spend it on tequila and cards and whores.''

''We fought valiantly,'' Manuel protested. ''I have the wounded arm to prove it.''

Deke's hand made a small, seemingly involuntary movement toward the gun holstered on his hip. ''I ought to shoot you both right now.''

Manuel flinched slightly, and Grady looked about ready to shit in his pants, thought Longarm.

Deke took a deep breath to bring his anger under control, and jerked a thumb at Scott. ''What about this hombre? Who's he?''

''He gave us a hand—'' Grady began.

Manuel interrupted him. ''He rode in with the two lawmen, but he did not take part in the fight. When it was over, he drew his guns and disarmed them, keeping them from killing Grady and me in cold blood.''

Coffin exploded. ''We ain't murderers like you, greaser! We don't shoot men down like dogs—even when they deserve it!''

Deke silenced Coffin with a short wave of his hand. ''Shut up.'' He looked at Scott. ''Seems like you've got some explaining to do.''

''Name's Walt Scott,'' the drifter said easily. ''I've heard of your bunch, and it sounds like the kind of organization I'd like to hook up with. I hear tell you come up with some pretty good money.''

''We get our share of loot,'' said Deke. ''But we're not running a haven for gunfighters. Why should we take you in?''

Scott gestured with his guns at Longarm and Coffin. ''I brought you a couple of lawmen to do with as you will.''

Deke laughed harshly. ''What are a pair of badge-toters worth?''

''You tell me. Anyway, Long and Coffin here are pretty smart fellas . . . most of the time. If I hadn't come along, they might've found this hideout and given you some real trouble,

Deke. They're looking for a girl, a Señorita Guiterrez they say you kidnapped back in Del Rio."

Longarm had remained silent as long as he could. "Where is she?" he asked sharply. "If you've hurt her—"

Deke jerked his gun out suddenly and stepped forward, making Manuel and Grady jump back in fright. Instead of threatening the outlaws, however, Deke brought the barrel of the revolver up and eared back its hammer as he lined the muzzle on Longarm's face. "Start threatening me, you son of a bitch," Deke grated, "and I'll blow your brains out right here and now—"

"Deke! Put that gun down."

The imperiously voiced command made Longarm's breath catch in his throat. Even though the muzzle of Deke's gun bore an uncanny resemblance to a cannon at this range, Longarm was able to tear his gaze away from it and look toward the door that led into the other room.

Sonia stood there, dressed in a low-cut gown the color of burnished copper, just like her hair. She held a glass of wine in one hand, a small pistol in the other. The glitter of mocking laughter danced in her dark eyes.

"This bastard was shootin' his mouth off," Deke began without looking back at her.

"I know Señor Long quite well," said Sonia, "and I am certain that his words were prompted only by concern for me. Misplaced, perhaps, but still concern."

"What the hell?" exclaimed Coffin.

Longarm wasn't as puzzled as the big Ranger was. The realization of what was really going on hit him like a fist in the gut, making a sour taste rise in his mouth. "El Aguila didn't kidnap you at all, did he, Sonia?" he said tautly. "It was all just an act. You came willingly."

She smiled at him. "You are a shrewd man, Custis."

"No, I'm a damned fool. Here I thought you were in danger from El Aguila, when all along you were working with him."

"Not exactly." Sonia took a sip of her wine. "You see, Custis, there is no El Aguila."

Chapter 13

"Or rather, there is," she went on, "but he has nothing to do with us."

Coffin shook his head. "I ain't understandin' this at all."

Longarm was. He said slowly, "You just used the name so that everybody would be more afraid of the gang. El Aguila's reputation carries some weight in the border country, doesn't it?"

"He is well known to be a fierce outlaw," Sonia said with a shrug that made her breasts bob slightly, intriguingly. Even under these circumstances, Longarm couldn't completely ignore the lush appeal of her body. "As you say, my men simply used his name."

"I thought it was sort of funny that a fella who'd always been known as a lone wolf would suddenly throw in with a bunch of owlhoots," said Coffin, scowling darkly. "I should'a knowed El Aguila wouldn't be runnin' with a gang of no-accounts like this."

Deke started to step forward again, his lips pulling back from his teeth in a grimace of hate, but Sonia stopped him with a look. "Say what you will, Señor Coffin," she told the big Ranger, "but you and Señor Long are still our prisoners."

She was right about that, thought Longarm. It didn't matter whether El Aguila was here or not. He and Coffin were still in deadly danger.

"Nobody's answered my question," Walt Scott put in. "Do I get to join up or not?"

"Señor . . . Scott, was it?" Sonia took another sip of her wine and sidled closer. Her gaze raked blatantly over Scott's tall, rangy figure. He wasn't a handsome man; his features were too rugged and powerful for that. But what Sonia saw seemed to meet with her approval. She reached out with the hand holding the wine glass and brushed a finger across the sleeve of Scott's shirt. He met her bold stare impassively.

"I think there may be a place for you in our organization, Señor Scott," Sonia went on after a moment. "You seem to me to be a resourceful man. Such a man could rise to a position of power."

Longarm glanced toward Deke. As he suspected, the second in command didn't look at all happy about the way Sonia was practically drooling over Scott. Deke's face was flushed with jealousy and anger. Longarm wondered just how many men Sonia thought she could keep under control with her sexual powers.

Sonia said to Scott, "Our leader will be here soon, and he will make the final decision regarding your presence in our stronghold. But for now . . . welcome, Señor Scott. I hope your stay is a pleasant one. I will do everything in my power to make it so."

"We'd better get these two locked up," Deke said sharply, gesturing with his gun toward Longarm and Coffin.

Reluctantly, Sonia took her attention away from Scott and turned toward the captive lawmen. "Yes, you are right, Deke. Make certain they are secure. Señor Long, I fear, could cause us a great deal of trouble, given the opportunity."

"What about me?" protested Coffin, sounding offended. "I'm dangerous too, damn it."

"Shut your mouth," Deke growled. He jabbed the air with the gun. "Get moving, both of you."

He indicated that they should leave the room by the same door through which he and Sonia had entered. Coffin went first, followed by Longarm, and as he walked out of the room, Longarm cast a final glance at Sonia. Her eyes met his for an instant, and he thought he saw something like regret there.

Then Deke moved between the two of them, cutting off Longarm's view of Sonia and shutting the door behind him.

They were in a hallway that led toward the rear of the big house. Several doors opened off the corridor, and as they passed one that was open, Deke spoke in Spanish to some men who were the side room. They came out, drawing their guns as they did so, and Longarm figured they were extra guards to keep an eye on him and Coffin while Deke was taking them wherever they were going. One of them carried a lantern.

While the other men covered Longarm and Coffin, Deke searched them, removing Longarm's matches and cheroots and the pocket watch with the derringer attached to the other end of the chain. Longarm just shrugged when Deke gave him a hard-eyed look.

He wasn't surprised when they left the house through a rear door and proceeded toward a smaller building set just inside the high adobe wall that ran around the entire place. The small, square, flat-roofed structure was made of sturdy logs and had only one door and no windows. Longarm knew a smokehouse when he saw one.

"We'll lock up the two of you inside there," said Deke, indicating the smokehouse with a jerk of his gun. "There's no way out. When the boss gets here, he'll know what to do with you." Deke gave an ugly laugh. "I'm betting you'll die, both of you."

"We'll see," said Longarm. "I've always believed in eating the apple one bite at a time."

"You're going to choke on this one," Deke predicted smugly. He holstered his gun, and while the other men covered Longarm and Coffin, he brought out a key and unlocked the heavy lock on the smokehouse door. When it was open, he stepped back so that the other outlaws could prod the two lawmen inside.

"Get a good night's sleep," Deke told them as he shut the door. "It might be your last."

The thick wooden door slammed shut with finality. A moment later, Longarm heard the lock click into place.

"Well, ain't this a fine howdy-do," Coffin said bitterly into the darkness. The inside of the smokehouse was stygian in its lack of light. "I reckon I owe you an apology, Long."

"How do you figure that?" asked Longarm.

"I was the one who invited Scott to join up with us. If it hadn't been for that low-down rabid skunk, we wouldn't be in this damn mess."

Longarm shrugged, even though he knew Coffin couldn't see him. "I might have done the same thing, especially after the way Scott took a hand in that fight with the Yaquis. He saved our lives."

"Only so that he could double-cross us later."

"Maybe. Maybe, like he said, he just saw an opportunity and took it."

Longarm wasn't sure whether he believed that or not. From his first glimpse of Scott, days earlier in Del Rio, he had sensed that there was something odd about the man, something dangerous. Scott had certainly proven Longarm's instincts correct.

In the brief glimpse Longarm had had inside the smokehouse while the lantern light illuminated it, he had seen that the little building was empty. It had looked as if a long time had passed since it had been used for smoking meat. Now Longarm extended a hand and moved carefully to the side until his fingertips brushed the rough wood of the wall. He sat down on the hard ground and leaned his back against the hard logs.

"Might as well get as comfortable as we can," he said to Coffin. "I reckon it's going to be a long night."

"Yeah," rumbled the big Ranger. Longarm heard faint noises as Coffin sat down. "Somethin' else is botherin' me," Coffin went on. "Deke and that gal both said something about the real boss of this outfit. What do you reckon they meant by that? Once we found out the real El Aguila wasn't mixed up with 'em, I figured Deke was runnin' things, or if not him, then the girl."

"I noticed that too," replied Longarm. "And I thought the same thing you did before they said that. There's something mighty strange going on here, Coffin. I don't think we've got the whole story yet."

"Me neither." Coffin chuckled. "Reckon we'll live long enough to figure it all out?"

"Your guess is as good as mine, old son," Longarm told him. "But we ain't dead yet."

Even though the circumstances weren't very conducive to sleep, both of the lawmen were exhausted and were unable to fight off slumber. Longarm heard loud, rattling snores coming from Coffin, and not even that could keep him awake. He dozed off moments later.

When he awoke, the tiny shafts of light slanting in through small chinks in the walls told him it was morning, and his neck was painfully stiff from leaning against the log wall all night. There was enough light in the smokehouse now for Longarm to see Coffin sprawled on the ground on the other side of the makeshift prison. The Ranger was stirring around and making snorting noises. Longarm climbed stiffly to his feet and stretched the best he could, considering the fact that his head brushed the low ceiling of the building. Then he said, "Coffin. Wake up, Coffin."

Grunting and grumbling, Coffin rolled over and blinked blearily up at Longarm. "Hey, we're still alive," he said, sounding surprised by that fact.

"For a while anyway." Longarm wondered if the outlaws were going to bring them any breakfast or just let them go hungry. His belly was rumbling from emptiness, and he could have used a few cups of coffee and a leisurely smoked cheroot too. He doubted if he was going to get any of those things.

Which meant he was surprised a few minutes later when the lock rattled and a voice called, "Step back away from the door in there. If you're anywhere close when I open up, there's a pair of shotguns out here that'll blast both of you to hell.''

Longarm didn't recognize the rough voice. When he and Coffin moved over to the far side of the smokehouse and the door swung open, he didn't know the bearded face that peered in at them either. It had to belong to one of the outlaws, though. The man was flanked by two more of the gang who held greeners pointed at Longarm and Coffin. They followed the bearded man inside, keeping the double barrels of the weapons pointed at the prisoners.

The big man was carrying a tray with a couple of tin cups, some chunks of bread, and a few slices of bacon on it. Longarm's mouth watered at the sight of the food.

''The señorita says that no matter what happens to you boys, we ain't goin' to starve you to death,'' said the bearded outlaw. He set the tray down on the ground and backed away from it. Reaching outside the door, he picked up a wooden bucket and set it on the floor inside as well. ''You got food and coffee, and you got a slops bucket.'' An evil grin split his weathered face. ''All the comforts of home, ain't it?''

''You goin' to shut up and let us eat,'' asked Coffin, ''or do you figure on jawin' at us all day?''

The bearded man waved a hand at the food. ''Go ahead, eat.'' He gave a cackle of laughter. ''Might be your last meal.''

Longarm sighed. He was getting mighty tired of folks saying things like that to him.

The outlaws backed out of the smokehouse, slammed the door behind them, and locked it. Longarm and Coffin dug in. The bread was stale and the bacon was cold, but neither man cared much about that. The coffee, at least, was hot, and strong too. Longarm drank it gratefully.

After they had polished off the crude breakfast and relieved themselves in the bucket, Longarm and Coffin retreated to the rear corners of the smokehouse and sat down again. ''Goin' to get mighty hot in here 'fore the day's over,'' commented Coffin.

Longarm nodded in agreement. ''Maybe we won't be in

here that long.'' Of course, he added to himself, that might not necessarily be a good thing. . . .

As it turned out, less than half an hour later, the door was unlocked and opened again. This time Deke stood there, his gun out, accompanied by several guards. ''All right, Coffin, come out of there,'' he snapped.

Both Coffin and Longarm stood up. Deke's gun swung over to point at Longarm. ''Not you,'' said the outlaw. ''Just Coffin.''

The two lawmen exchanged a glance. Neither of them knew what this development meant. The outlaws might be taking Coffin out to shoot him. On the other hand, splitting them up like this could mean that Longarm would be the first to die. There was no way of knowing.

But Coffin stuck his hand out anyway. ''Good workin' with you, Long,'' he said. ''Maybe we'll get a chance to do it again sometime.''

''Sure,'' Longarm agreed easily as he shook hands with the big man. ''*Vaya con Dios,* Coffin.''

''Come on, come on,'' Deke said disgustedly. ''I ain't got all day.''

Coffin gave Longarm a grin and stepped out of the smokehouse. Longarm watched as the guards began marching him toward the house. Then Deke slammed the door, and semidarkness closed in around Longarm once more.

It didn't last long. A little later, as he was sitting against the rear wall again, he heard footsteps pause outside the smokehouse. When a key rattled in the lock, he squinted his eyes against the glare he knew would fall through the entrance when the door was opened. Sure enough, the door swung back and a figure stood there, starkly silhouetted against the brilliance of the sun.

Only one person in this outlaw stronghold had a shape like that, Longarm thought.

Sonia stepped inside and pulled the door shut behind her. Longarm's eyes had already started to adjust to the glare, and for a moment he couldn't see her clearly. Then, as his vision returned to its usual sharpness, he could make out the white shirt she wore and the denim trousers that snugly hugged her hips and thighs. ''Been riding?'' he asked.

''Not yet,'' she said as she came closer to him.

Longarm didn't stand up. ''What do you want?''

''I came to see you, Custis, to make sure that you are being treated well.''

''What happened to Coffin?''

Sonia looked and sounded slightly impatient as she said, ''He is in the house with Deke and some of the other men. He has not been harmed, Custis. Do not worry about him.''

Longarm shook his head. ''I don't understand. What was the point of splitting us up?''

Sonia's hands went to the buttons of her shirt. ''I did not think you would like to make love to me with the Ranger watching. Of course, if you prefer it that way, I do not mind. It would not be the first time I have made love with people watching.'' She spread the shirt open, revealing her large, coral-tipped breasts.

Despite his anger at Sonia and the entire situation, Longarm felt a quickening in his groin at the sight of her body. Still not getting up, he said, ''You risked coming in here alone with me just so we could fool around a mite?''

''There is no risk,'' she said casually. ''Inside the house, so that they cannot hear what we do, are four men with rifles trained on the door of this smokehouse. If anyone other than myself opens that door, they will open fire. So you see, Custis, no matter what you do to me, you still cannot escape.'' She gave him a sultry smile. ''So you might as well do something that we will both enjoy, no?''

She took the shirt all the way off and dropped it at her feet. Her hands went to her breasts, cupping and kneading them, caressing them as a lover would. As her thumbs stroked the erect nipples, her hips began to sway enticingly back and forth.

Longarm's throat was dry, and his breath seemed to clog inside it. He knew now the kind of woman Sonia was, knew that she was thick as thieves, so to speak, with these outlaws. She had used him, then been responsible for him and Coffin winding up in this death trap.

But she was still one hell of a woman, and God help him, he wanted her.

She reached down to her waist, unfastened the trousers, pushed them down over her hips. She wore nothing under them, and Longarm saw beads of moisture sparkling in the thick triangle of dark hair between her thighs. Sonia kicked her boots off, then the pants, and stood completely naked before Longarm. Parting her legs slightly, she reached between them with her right hand and began stroking herself. After a moment, as her breathing became harder and harsher in her throat, she lowered herself into a crouch. With her legs spread wide as she balanced on her heels, Longarm could see plainly as she plunged her middle finger into the folds of female flesh.

"You could do this . . . much better, Custis," she said breathlessly.

Longarm had a difficult time getting the words out, but he managed to say, "I thought you liked it when folks watched you."

She closed her eyes and began stroking and thrusting harder, pumping her hips back and forth with wanton abandon. Longarm's manhood was like a thick length of iron bar by now. Sensation throbbed through it as he watched Sonia bring herself closer and closer to a climax.

Suddenly, she threw herself forward at him. Longarm grabbed her, pulling her against him so that his mouth could crash against hers. Her fingers, still wet with her own juices, fumbled desperately with his belt and the buttons of his trousers. There was no gentleness here, only raw, naked need. Longarm lifted his hips enough for her to push his trousers and long underwear down, and as his fully erect shaft bobbed up, Sonia impaled herself on it without hesitation. She clasped her thighs tightly around his hips and stuck her tongue deep in his mouth as she began rocking back and forth, her channel filled with him.

Longarm thrust up from beneath her. His left hand cupped her right breast while his right reached around behind her to squeeze the cheeks of her bottom. Sonia moaned as she bounced up and down wildly on him. It was all Longarm could do to make sure he remained deeply socketed inside her.

The end came quickly, as he knew it would. With one final thrust, he began to spew his seed in her, even as spasm after spasm rippled strongly through her, shaking her as if the ground itself had begun to heave and buck. Maybe it had, a part of Longarm's lust-stunned brain told him. Earthquakes sometimes occurred in this part of Mexico, didn't they?

The movement of the earth was only in his imagination, he realized a moment later as he slumped back against the wall of the smokehouse, drained and sated. The ground was steady underneath him. Little tremors were still running through Sonia's body, though.

"You are . . . much man . . . Custis," she was able to say after a couple of minutes. "I will . . . miss you."

Longarm cupped her chin and tilted her head back so that he could look into her eyes. Whatever tender feelings he might have had toward her were gone, driven away by the knowledge of who and what she really was. But there was one thing he wanted to know. "Back in Del Rio, just before the raid . . . why did you take me into that alley?"

"Why . . . because I wanted to, of course." She looked at him as if she couldn't believe he had asked such a foolish question.

And now that he thought about it, neither could he.

Sonia Guiterrez took what she wanted. Always.

Chapter 14

A few minutes after Sonia had left the smokehouse, Coffin was brought back, escorted by Deke and a couple of other men. Deke planted his hand in the middle of Coffin's back and gave the Ranger a hard shove that sent him stumbling into the little building. Deke laughed. Coffin caught his balance and righted himself, then swung around with a thunderous scowl on his face and his hands balled into fists. He looked as if he was ready to ignore the guns pointed at him and throw himself at Deke.

Longarm stepped forward and took hold of Coffin's arm. "No point in giving them a good excuse to ventilate you," he told Coffin in a low, urgent voice. "We'll stand a better chance of getting out of here if we keep our heads."

"You won't be getting out of here, either of you," said Deke. "It doesn't matter how the girl feels about you, Long, you'll still die. I figure as soon as the boss gets here, he'll give us the go-ahead to get rid of you. We've got some boys riding with us who're part Yaqui. They'll have a fine time working you over with their knives, and then we'll throw your bodies in a gully at the far end of the valley. The coyotes and the *zopilotes* will have a good time too."

Longarm tried not to think about coyotes and buzzards and

other scavengers. He tugged Coffin over to the rear wall of the smokehouse. The big Ranger went reluctantly. Longarm knew he was making an effort not to lose his temper.

The door slammed shut. Deke snapped the padlock back on the hasp and laughed again, the sound fading as he walked away from the smokehouse. Longarm let go of Coffin's arm and asked, "What did they do to you in there?"

"Just knocked me around a mite," replied Coffin. Longarm could see bruises starting to form on the Ranger's face, and a small cut over Coffin's left eye oozed blood. "It didn't amount to much. I been hit a lot harder in friendly fights. Hell, you walloped me better'n this when we were tusslin' over Anna Marie back in Del Rio."

The mention of Anna Marie made Longarm think of the fiery redhead. She was a whore who worked in a border-town saloon, while Sonia Guiterrez had all the advantages of wealth and breeding and a father who was in a position of power. Yet there was no question in Longarm's mind which of the women was more respectable.

"We got to start thinkin' of some way to get out of here," Coffin went on. "I'd still like to take that gal back to Del Rio, just so's I could dump her at her pa's feet and tell him just how low-down she really is. Or you reckon he knows already?"

Longarm thought about the things Capitan Hernandez of the *federales* had told him about Sonia. "No, Don Alfredo doesn't know," he said. "He won't allow himself to know. I reckon that's the only way he can handle it."

"Well, I might feel sorry for the poor son of a bitch—if it hadn't been him who sent us down here and got us into this mess in the first place."

"Can't blame the man for being worried about his daughter," Longarm pointed out. "Remember, we thought she'd been kidnapped by El Aguila too."

A short bark of laughter escaped from the Ranger. "You reckon wherever the real El Aguila is, he knows that this bunch has been usin' his name?"

"No telling," said Longarm with a shake of his head. "But if I was him, I wouldn't be too happy about it."

With a sigh, Coffin sat down on the dirt floor and leaned against the log wall. "Well, I reckon now we wait some more . . . unless you've got some ideas about how we might get out of here."

"Not yet," said Longarm. "Besides, I'm sort of interested in finding out just who the real boss of this setup is."

"You mean we ought to wait until he shows up 'fore we make our move?"

"The thought occurred to me," admitted Longarm.

"I hope you're right, Long. We best get out of here mighty quick-like after that, though, or else we'll wind up with some o' them Yaqui halfbreeds peelin' our skin off in inch-wide strips."

The hours passed as slowly as any Longarm could remember. None of the outlaws brought food or water to them at midday, and by late afternoon Longarm's stomach was rumbling loudly from emptiness and his mouth was dry and parched. The heat in the smokehouse wrapped around him like a living thing and made him gasp for breath. Coffin was just as uncomfortable, but while the federal lawman suffered in silence, the Ranger gave vent to his spleen in a never-ending stream of muttered curses. Longarm got used to the sound, and actually fell asleep to it.

He woke up abruptly only a few minutes later when Coffin said sharply, "There's somebody comin', Long."

Longarm sat up. He heard the footsteps approaching the smokehouse too, and a moment after they stopped right outside the door, a key rattled in the lock. The door was pulled open, and as usual, Longarm and Coffin were left squinting and blinking against the glare.

"Come on out of there," ordered Deke, and even though they couldn't see him very well against the brightness of the sunshine, the tone of his voice made it clear that he was holding a gun on them.

Longarm stood up and stepped out of the smokehouse, followed by Coffin. Longarm's eyes were adjusting to the light by now, and he saw Deke standing several feet away, six-gun leveled just as Longarm had expected. Four more of the outlaws accompanied the man.

"Time to go inside," Deke said. "Somebody wants to see you boys."

Longarm didn't like the tone of amusement in Deke's voice. If the outlaw was that happy about something, it couldn't bode very well for the two prisoners. As they started walking toward the house, with a couple of the men flanking them and Deke and the other guards following closely behind, Longarm said, "The boss must be here."

"Must be," said Deke, still sounding cheerful.

Longarm and Coffin exchanged a wary glance. They hadn't been able to work out a suitable escape plan, but the meaning in each man's eyes was clear: They had run out of time, and if either of them saw even the slightest opportunity for escape, they should seize it without hesitation.

They were taken in through the rear door of the house, then escorted down the same corridor by which they had left it. Their destination was obviously the same large comfortably furnished room in which they had first confronted Deke and Sonia.

Sonia was in that room now, Longarm saw as the door was opened and he and Coffin were prodded through it. She stood next to the fireplace, wearing another expensive gown that hugged her lush figure and showed off its appeal. A man in a dark gray suit was standing beside her, his back to the newcomers.

Longarm recognized the man anyway. He should have been shocked, he supposed, but he really wasn't.

"Here they are," Deke said, and Franklin Barton turned from where he stood beside Sonia to smile arrogantly at Longarm and Coffin.

"Son of a bitch!" exclaimed Coffin. "It's that diplomat fella!"

"Indeed it is," said Barton smoothly. "I'm glad you remember me, Mr. Coffin."

"It's only been a few days, Barton," Longarm said. "I reckon it'd take longer than that for us to forget a skunk like you."

For a moment, Barton's eyes turned hard and cold and his jaw tightened. Then he relaxed and gave a dry chuckle. "Well, we can certainly all see that *you're* not a diplomat, Marshal Long."

"Never claimed to be. I'm just a fella who tries to do his job."

"So am I." Barton waved a hand, the gesture encompassing the room as well as Sonia and Deke. "And my real job is here."

"You mean you're the one who's ramroddin' this gang?" asked Coffin, his expression a mixture of anger and amazement.

"Indeed I am."

"But . . . why?" This time puzzlement won out on Coffin's bearded face.

Barton reached over to Sonia, taking her hand and lifting it momentarily to his lips before he turned back to the captive lawmen. "Isn't it obvious? What man wouldn't betray even those closest to him for a beautiful creature such as this?"

"The two of you met in Arizona last year, didn't you?" guessed Longarm. "You were with the Vice-President, Barton, and Sonia was with her father."

"You are a smart man, Custis," said Sonia. "You have figured it all out, no?"

"Maybe not all of it," Longarm said slowly, "but I reckon I'm on the right trail."

Barton smirked at him. "Then why don't you tell us all about it?"

Anything to keep their captors from killing him and Coffin for a while, Longarm thought. He said, "You didn't want Coffin and me coming down here after Sonia because you knew she hadn't really been kidnapped. Grabbing her in Del Rio was just one more part of your scheme."

"But of course Don Alfredo wouldn't be dissuaded from the idea, so I had no choice but to go along with him and hope that the two of you would meet a bad end down here south of the border," said Barton. "As you soon will. But go ahead, I didn't mean to interrupt."

"Seems to me like what you've probably got in mind is

to make Don Alfredo pay a big ransom to El Aguila in order to get his daughter back alive and unharmed.''

Barton nodded. ''Excellent reasoning. For a price, Guiterrez will get Sonia back as pure and untouched as she was when she was taken from Del Rio.''

Longarm supposed that statement was true enough, even though Barton didn't mean it the way Don Alfredo would likely take it.

''That's it?'' asked Longarm. ''This whole scheme was just to bilk some money out of Don Alfredo?''

''Of course not. The important part is where that money will go,'' Sonia said proudly. ''It will go to help free Mexico from the iron hand of the corrupt dictator Diaz and his lackeys such as my father.''

''That sounds like revolution talk to me,'' said Longarm.

''It is!'' Some of the same fire he had seen in Sonia's eyes during their lovemaking burned in her gaze now as she stepped toward him. ''Soon the government my father represents will be nothing but a bitter memory in the minds of the Mexican people.''

Longarm had crossed paths with Porfirio Diaz in the past, and held no affection for the Mexican president. In fact, the two of them had been outright enemies, and nothing would have pleased El Presidente more than the death of the man known south of the border as El Brazo Largo.

But that didn't mean Longarm wanted to see Diaz overthrown when it would also mean that Franklin Barton would get away with betraying his own country. Longarm figured that Barton's interest in revolution was more financial than political, so he said skeptically, ''You're not getting anything out of this, Barton?''

''Oh, I'll be well compensated in the end,'' Barton admitted, ''both by the favors of Señorita Guiterrez here and the gratitude of the new ruling party. You see, Long, there's more to this than simply getting Don Alfredo to ransom his daughter. There's also going to be trouble between our government and Mexico, because that will further weaken Diaz.''

"So you plan to sabotage the border negotiations," Longarm said grimly.

Coffin seemed to be catching on. He growled at Barton, "That's why you was bein' such a pain in the ass about everything back in Del Rio."

"Very perceptive of you, Mr. Coffin, and of course you too, Marshal Long." Barton looked so pleased with himself that Longarm wanted to fling himself across the room and wipe that smug expression off the treacherous diplomat's face. Longarm controlled the impulse.

"So the two of you hatched this whole scheme last year when you met in Inferno." It was more of a statement than a question.

Sonia nodded. "As soon as I met Franklin, I knew he was *muy simpatico* to my goals."

Coffin grunted and said, "What fella wouldn't be if he thought goin' along with you would get him in your pants?"

Barton frowned. "There's no need to be crude, Mr. Coffin," he snapped.

Maybe a wedge could be driven between the plotters, thought Longarm. He said, "Doesn't it bother you, Barton, that while Sonia's using you, she's jumping into bed with damn near every other man she meets?"

Barton shook his head and said, "Not at all. I'm well aware of the, ah, capacity of Sonia's appetites. No one man could ever satisfy all of them." He slid an arm around her waist and pulled her closer to him so that he could reach up and stroke her breast through the gown. Sonia smiled and practically purred as she snuggled against his side. "But we both know who she really loves," Barton went on.

It was a bold statement, but Barton was just deluding himself, Longarm thought. Somewhere deep down, Barton probably knew that too. But the fantasy that Sonia was really in love with him, plus the money that he stood to make on this deal, would be enough for Barton. It would have to be.

"What about El Aguila?" asked Longarm, still stalling for time. "What's his part in this?"

"I told you, he has no part," replied Sonia. "Our men

merely used his name during their raids and made certain that it was overheard.''

"So you had a ready-made scapegoat if anything went wrong. The law would be looking for El Aguila, when it was really Deke here who rounded up the gang and led them on their raids.''

"That's right,'' Deke said, as satisfied with himself as Barton and Sonia both were. "And I'm getting a good payoff too, Long.''

"How often does Sonia visit *your* bunk?''

"That's enough,'' Barton said sharply. "I don't care about the past, but now that I'm here, things will be different.''

Longarm thought Deke's jaw was a little more taut than it had been before Barton's bold statement, but he couldn't be sure. Anyway, it looked as if trying to cause friction between Barton and Deke over Sonia was a lost cause. Lust was one thing, but for some men, money could make up for a lot of lonely, frustrated nights.

"Take them back out to the smokehouse and lock them up,'' Barton continued. "We'll deal with them later.''

Deke frowned. "I figured we'd go ahead and kill 'em now.''

"I said later.'' An ugly smile tugged at Barton's mouth under the mustache. "Condemned men deserve a last meal. Mr. Coffin and Marshal Long will dine with us this evening.''

Sonia and Deke both looked surprised by Barton's order, but neither of them argued the point. Deke drew his gun and started toward Longarm and Coffin, obviously intending to prod them from the room and take them back to their makeshift prison.

"Wait a minute,'' Longarm said quickly. "What about that fella Scott?''

"Yeah,'' growled Coffin. "If I'm goin' to die, there's a few things I'd like to say to that double-crossin' bastard first.''

"Save them until dinner,'' Barton said. "I intend to ask Mr. Scott to join us.''

"Just for the meal," asked Longarm, "or is he part of the gang now?"

"We'll see. I *do* owe him a debt of thanks for delivering the two of you to us. I believe you would have caused no end of trouble had not fortune—and Mr. Scott—placed you in our hands."

"You're damned right about that," said Coffin.

"Shut up and get moving," snapped Deke.

Menaced by the guns in the hands of Deke and the other guards, Longarm and Coffin had no choice but to walk slowly from the room and along the corridor to the rear door of the house. They were taken back to the little log building and shoved inside. Deke stood just outside the door, and as he sneered in at them, the last rays of the setting sun touched his face and turned it a hellish red.

"This next meal really will be your last one," he said. "You won't be alive to see the sun come up in the morning."

"We'll still be breathin' when you're nothin' but a corpse crawlin' with maggots," Coffin blustered.

Deke's finger tightened on the trigger of the gun he was pointing at the Ranger, but he stopped the motion short of firing. An ugly laugh came from him. "Say whatever you want if it makes you feel better," he said as he reached out to grasp the door. "You'll still be just as dead later on."

The door slammed shut, plunging the two lawmen into a thick gloom.

But the darkness inside the smokehouse wasn't as deep as that of the grave, thought Longarm. He and Coffin had survived another test, and they were still alive.

They still had a chance.

Chapter 15

The night was a beautiful one. The heat of the day had begun to fade when Longarm and Coffin were taken from the smokehouse and marched toward the hacienda. A cool breeze laden with the scents of pine and wildflowers brushed their faces. Normally, the prospect of sharing dinner with a beautiful woman on a night like this would have Longarm's brain turning to thoughts of passion.

But tonight he might as well have been dining in a nest of rattlesnakes. His muscles were taut as he and Coffin were taken down another hallway to a big dining room on the far side of the house. They hadn't been there before.

French doors opened from the dining room onto a patio that was bordered with flower beds, and the scent of flowers was even stronger there. It was mixed with the delicious aromas emanating from the platters of food on the long hardwood table in the center of the room. Heavy chairs with high, elaborately carved wooden backs were lined along the sides of the table. Franklin Barton sat at the end, in the place of honor. On his right was Deke, to his left was Sonia. The other chairs were vacant except for one on the left side, near the far end from Barton's place.

Walt Scott sat there.

The drifter lounged in the chair, the long, slender fingers of his left hand toying with the stem of the wine glass in front of him. A cigar just like the ones Barton and Deke were smoking was between the fingers of his right hand, the red coal on its tip smoldering. Scott seemed to be at ease and completely pleased with himself.

"Good evening, gentlemen," Barton greeted Longarm and Coffin. "So nice of you to join us. Sit wherever you like."

Longarm pulled out a chair across from Scott, but Coffin hesitated. "I don't want to sit where I have to look at this son of a bitch," he said with a gesture toward Scott. "We wouldn't be here if it wasn't for him."

"Probably all too true," agreed Barton. Scott didn't seem to be offended by Coffin's blunt statement. A faint grin tugged at the corners of his mouth.

"Just sit down, Coffin," Longarm told the Ranger. He glanced at the other places set at the table. "Looks like you're having even more company."

"Some of dear Sonia's associates will be riding in this evening," said Barton. "I thought it would only be polite to ask them to join us once they arrive. However, if you're worried about the delay, I suppose we could go ahead and begin dinner. After all, the sooner we're finished, the sooner we can go on to other matters."

Coffin sat down on the same side of the table as Scott and Deke, about halfway between the two men. He exchanged a glance with Longarm. They both knew what Barton meant. The sooner dinner was over, the sooner the two prisoners would be turned over to the outlaws with Yaqui blood in them to be tortured.

"I don't reckon we're in any hurry," Longarm said dryly. "We can wait for the other guests."

Barton puffed on his cigar and then blew smoke to the side. "Somehow I thought you might feel that way," he said. "In the meantime, would you care for some wine?"

"I could use a real drink," declared Coffin. "Got any whiskey?"

Barton sighed. "I try to bring a little culture into the proceedings, and this is my thanks. Of course we have whiskey,

Mr. Coffin. I'll have one of the servants fetch some for you." Barton turned and flipped a hand at an elderly Mexican man who was standing near the door of the dining room. The man nodded and slipped out of the room.

Longarm didn't see any other servants, but there were a couple of gunmen standing guard, one near the doors that led out to the patio, the other leaning against the wall a few feet away from the end of the table where Longarm and Scott were sitting. Longarm and Coffin had been disarmed, of course, and with the two outlaws, Deke, Scott, and Barton all in the room and no doubt carrying guns, the odds were awfully high. However, they would get even higher when the Mexican revolutionaries arrived and joined them. If he and Coffin were going to at least die fighting, they would have to make their move soon. When Longarm met Coffin's eyes for a second, he could tell that the big Ranger felt the same way.

Before either of them could do anything, the door opened again and a young man carrying a bottle of whiskey and a tray with two glasses on it glided into the room. This servant was a different one, and it was obvious that the old man had sent him to fetch the whiskey and bring it into the dining room. Longarm didn't remember seeing the young man around the hacienda before, but that didn't mean anything. The gang could have several of the local people working for them, doing menial tasks. This youngster wore the white shirt and trousers and rope-soled sandals of a peasant farmer, which was probably exactly what he was most of the time.

"Ah, here's your whiskey, Mr. Coffin," said Barton with a smile, playing the good host. "Would you care for some, Marshal Long, or would you prefer wine? I should have asked you before now."

"That's all right," said Longarm. "I think I'll have some of that wine."

"Excellent." Barton looked around for the elderly Mexican. "Blast it, where did Pablo go? I was going to have him pour." With a sigh, Barton scraped his chair back and stood up. "I suppose I'll have to do it myself."

He took a step toward a bucket of water in which the bottle

of wine sat, then stopped short as a crash of glass filled the room.

Longarm's eyes jerked toward the young servant, who was still clutching the bottle of whiskey but who had dropped the tray containing the two glasses. They were what had shattered on the tile floor. The young man was staring, wide-eyed, in awe. His mouth moved, and he uttered hoarsely, "El Aguila! *Sí*, it is really you!"

He was looking straight at Walt Scott.

Longarm studied Scott through narrowed eyes. Scott laid the cigar on the table, being careful not to place the burning end against the wood where it would scorch the polished surface. He was still outwardly calm, but his fingers had tightened on the stem of the wine glass. Longarm wouldn't have been surprised if the crystal had suddenly snapped into half. Scott drew a deep breath and said to the servant, "I think you're mistaken, son."

"No, no, señor!" protested the young man. "I would never forget you after the way you helped us when those evil men tried to take my father's farm on the Rio Grande. All along the river, the kindness of El Aguila is legend to the common people!"

Barton leaned forward, his hands flat on the table. His voice lashed out. "Well, Scott, what about it? Is this true?"

A lazy smile drifted across Walt Scott's face as he said, "Reckon it is."

That was the last lazy thing to happen for several moments.

Scott was on his feet in an instant, the long-barreled, black-handled Colts snaking out of their holsters as he pivoted toward the closest guard. He lashed out with the right-hand gun, taking the startled outlaw by surprise. The barrel raked across the man's forehead, opening a bloody gash and stunning him.

At the same time, Coffin lunged from his chair and tackled Deke, who was also trying to get up. They went down with a crash.

That left the guard by the patio doors for Longarm. The outlaw was further away from Longarm than either of the other two men had been from Scott and Coffin. He had time to draw his gun before Longarm could reach him. Longarm grabbed desperately for the weapon as he threw himself forward. He got hold of the barrel with one hand and wrenched it aside, at the same time jamming his other hand between the hammer and the cylinder so that the gun couldn't fire. The hammer pinched the web of his hand painfully. Longarm let go of the gun barrel with his other hand and brought his fist across in a slashing blow that caught the outlaw in the jaw.

While Longarm was struggling with the last guard, Scott pivoted smoothly away from the unconscious outlaw on the floor and turned to face Sonia and Barton. The hammers of both guns were eared back. "If either of you let out a peep," he told them grimly, "I won't have any reason not to kill you both." His gray eyes were like chips of ice in the light of the chandelier hanging from the ceiling over the big table. "Take that gun out of the holster under your coat, Barton, put it on the table, and slide it down here."

Barton's face was set in lines of fury, but he complied with Scott's orders while Sonia looked stunned by the unexpected developments. Some thudding and bumping came from underneath the table, where Coffin and Deke had rolled in their struggle. Coffin suddenly appeared, raising himself up and lifting his right fist while he used his left hand to pin Deke down. The big fist fell, rose, fell again. A gurgling sound came from under the table. Coffin pushed himself to his feet. "Reckon that'll hold that fella for a while," he said in satisfaction.

Longarm, meanwhile, had yanked the pistol away from the last guard. He slammed the gun against the man's temple and heard the brittle crack of bone. The outlaw's knees folded up, and he collapsed on the floor with rivulets of blood leaking from his nose and ears. He was either dead or soon would be. Longarm turned back toward the table and lifted the gun he had taken from the guard.

Coffin was on the far side of the table, still breathing a little hard from his fight with Deke. Scott stood at the far end, guns trained on Barton and Sonia. Between them were the platters of food, forgotten now in this twist of fate. The young servant was gone, having slipped out in the confusion. Longarm hoped he wouldn't raise the alarm. Considering the way the boy had looked at Scott with an almost worshipful gaze, Longarm thought that was a distinct possibility.

"You're El Aguila?" Barton asked in a choked voice. "The real El Aguila?"

"That's right," said Scott. "That's what folks along the border got in the habit of calling me anyway, and I never disabused 'em of the notion." Without taking his eyes off Barton and Sonia, he went on. "I owe an apology to you, Marshal Long, and to you too, Ranger Coffin. I know it was pretty low-down of me to use you like that to get into this stronghold, but I wanted to find out who was muddying up my name."

"So you damn near got us killed," Coffin said harshly.

"I wouldn't have let anything happen to you," Scott said. "I've just been biding my time, waiting for the right moment to free the two of you so that we can get out of here." His broad shoulders rose and fell in a shrug. "The way things worked out, I didn't have much of a choice about when to start the ball."

Longarm wasn't completely sure if he should be pointing his gun toward Barton and Sonia or Scott. "What do you intend to do now?" he asked.

"You may not believe this, Marshal, but just because I've got a reputation as an outlaw, that doesn't mean I'll stand by and watch my country being betrayed by a man who's supposed to be representing its best interests. I think we should get out of here and take these two with us, back to Texas where they can face justice."

Scott's deep, resonant voice certainly sounded sincere enough, but Longarm had trusted Scott before, with nearly disastrous results. "What about you? Are you going to turn yourself in too?"

"You probably won't believe this either, but I haven't broken any laws, Marshal. At least not in Texas. There's been plenty of talk, but you won't find any reward dodgers out on me."

"The hell you say!" exclaimed Coffin. "I've heard about you, mister, heard how you like to horn in on every crooked scheme you come across."

"But did you ever see a wanted poster on me?" Scott persisted. "I don't think so."

They didn't have time for this argument, Longarm thought. He said, "It looks like we're going to have to trust you again for the time being, Scott, at least until we get out of here. But I'll be keeping a close eye on you."

"Wouldn't expect anything else from the fella they call Longarm," Scott said easily.

"You know who I am?"

"I make it my business to keep up with all the lawmen I can. Never know when I'll run across one."

"Well, you won't be running across any more unless we get out of here before those revolutionaries show up," said Longarm. "It'll be hard enough just slipping out with all of El Aguila's gang around."

Scott winced a little. "Please, Marshal. You're besmirching my reputation."

"When we get back to Texas, I'll smirch you, you low-down—" Coffin began.

"Let it wait," Longarm interrupted. "Coffin, you reckon you can slip out through that patio, get to the stable, and bring back horses for the five of us?"

"Damn right I can," the Ranger replied. He bent over and jerked a pistol from the holster strapped around the waist of the still-unconscious Deke. "Feels good not to be naked no more."

"Don't use that gun unless you have to," Scott warned. "Shots will bring everybody in the valley down on top of us."

"I know that, blast it," Coffin muttered. Moving with surprising stealth for a man of his size, he cat-footed out the door and vanished into the shadows of the patio.

"Now what?" Barton asked, his face impassive.

"Now we wait," Longarm said as he pointed his gun at the diplomat, "and hope nobody comes along and makes us shoot you. I'd a whole lot rather see you hang back in the States.''

Barton gave a contemptuous sniff, as if he thought that was unlikely to ever happen. Longarm had to admit that the odds against it were steep. To get Barton back to Texas, they would first have to escape from this outlaw stronghold, then make a long, perilous ride across the wasteland between the mountains and the border, probably being chased the whole way by the rest of the gang.

But if there was any way to bring Barton to justice, he was going to do it, Longarm vowed.

''There's only one way out of this valley that I know of,'' Scott said to Longarm, ''and if any of those outlaws get between us and the gap, they can block us off. We need some sort of distraction to draw them away.''

''I was thinking the same thing,'' Longarm agreed. ''Any ideas?''

''I happened to see a box of dynamite in the storehouse, like the raiders used to blow up Sheriff Sanderson's office in Del Rio. If we got hold of a few sticks of that stuff, and if one of us rode to the other end of the valley and set them off, that would draw the attention of all the outlaws. It might even be enough of a disturbance to draw the guards away from the gap.''

''But that man wouldn't have a chance to get away,'' Longarm pointed out. ''He'd be sacrificing his life.''

''Not if there's actually another way out of the valley.'' Scott looked intently at Barton, who was standing at the other end of the table with one hand on Sonia's shoulder. ''What about it, Barton? I've never seen an outlaw hideout without a back door. Where's the one in this valley?''

Barton laughed harshly. ''There isn't one, you fool. And if there was, do you think I'd tell you?''

''I don't have a whole lot to lose by killing you right here and now,'' Scott said grimly.

Barton just shook his head. ''You'll have to, because I'm not telling you anything.''

The soft clop of hoofbeats sounded outside the patio door. Longarm swung in that direction while Scott kept Sonia and

Barton covered. A moment later, Coffin's bulky figure appeared in the doorway. "I've got horses outside for the five of us," he announced. "Scott, that black devil of yours nipped a hunk out of my hide."

Scott smiled faintly. "Phantom's a one-man horse. He doesn't care much for other people messing with him."

"You're lucky I didn't throw your saddle on another hoss instead of riskin' life and limb the way I did." Coffin came farther into the dining room and peered down at Deke. "This old boy's still out cold, I see."

"You hit him pretty hard," said Longarm. "You may have killed him."

"Good riddance," muttered Coffin. "Now, how are we goin' to go about gettin' out of here?"

"Scott and I were just talking about that. We need a diversion to clear the way to the gap in the wall around this place."

Scott said, "I suggested that I set off a few sticks of dynamite up at the far end of the canyon."

Coffin grunted. "Might as well put a gun to your head and pull the trigger. You'd never get out alive."

"We don't know that. And it's worth a try, don't you think? You and Marshal Long can take Barton and Señorita Guiterrez back to Texas that way."

"Well, you're about the oddest owlhoot I've ever run across," said Coffin, "offerin' to give up your own life to save ours that way."

"Maybe we should draw straws to see who takes the dynamite," Longarm suggested.

Scott smiled again. "I'm the one who knows where it is. And besides, as Ranger Coffin pointed out earlier, I'm the one who got us into this." With a smooth movement, he holstered his guns and started toward the patio door, pausing only long enough to pick up his hat from a side table and settle it on his head. "Give me ten minutes."

With that he was gone, vanishing into the shadows outside.

"Damn it," grated Coffin. "You reckon we can trust that hombre, Long?"

"I don't see that we've got much choice," Longarm replied. He moved toward the end of the table. "On your feet, Sonia."

Her lovely features contorted with hate until they were anything but beautiful. "You will never get away with this, Custis," she said, practically spitting the words at him. "Turning you over to the Yaquis is too good for you. We will hang you from your feet and let you roast in the sun."

Longarm ignored the threat and motioned with the gun in his hand for Sonia to stand up. She did so reluctantly.

"There's no need for all these melodramatics, gentlemen," Barton said suddenly. "There's plenty of money to be made in this arrangement, plenty to go around for everyone. All you have to do is put up those guns and join us."

Coffin grinned. "Sounds to me like this fella's startin' to get a mite scared, Long. You reckon he figures there's a chance we might actually get him back to Texas to face a hang-rope?"

"Could be," said Longarm.

Barton's face was pale and taut. "Come now," he insisted, "how much does either of you make in a year's time? Give up this ridiculous idea and I can promise you ten times as much."

Longarm shook his head. "Might as well forget about it, Barton. Money's mighty nice, but there's some things it won't buy."

"That's preposterous—" the renegade diplomat began, but Coffin interrupted him.

"How long's Scott been gone?" asked the Ranger.

"Almost long enough," Longarm replied. He started toward the patio door. "Come on, you two," he said to Barton and Sonia. "By the time we all get mounted up, it'll be time to go."

"Custis, please," begged Sonia. "If I ever meant anything to you . . ."

"You meant just as much to me," Longarm said coldly, "as I meant to you."

Again her face twisted in a snarl as her true feelings were revealed. Under the threat of Longarm's gun, she started slowly toward the door. Barton moved alongside her.

That was when Deke surged up from the floor and leaped toward Coffin, grabbing the big Ranger's gun arm and thrusting it toward the ceiling. "Get the marshal, Barton!" Deke shouted.

Barton had no intention of tackling Longarm physically, though. As Longarm swung instinctively toward the fight between Coffin and Deke, Barton grabbed Sonia's arm, shoved her at Longarm, then threw himself toward the long table. Scott had left the diplomat's pistol lying on the far end. While Longarm struggled with Sonia, who was trying to claw his eyes out, Barton slid full-length along the polished wood, scattering the platters of food and reaching out to close his hand around the butt of the gun.

Over the shoulder of the cursing, spitting Sonia, Longarm saw Barton reach the pistol and twist back toward him. Silence was no longer an option. Longarm backhanded Sonia, knocking her to the side, and jerked up the pistol in his other hand. He and Barton fired at the same time, the mingled explosions deafening in the low-ceilinged room.

Longarm was accustomed to standing up in the face of enemy fire. Barton wasn't. The slug from Barton's gun whined harmlessly past Longarm's head to thud into the far wall. Longarm's bullet ripped into Barton and flung him backward off the table. Barton gave one brief cry of pain before he slammed into the floor and lay still and quiet, blood pooling under his side.

Deke still had hold of Coffin's gun arm, holding the weapon away from him. But Coffin's other hand was wrapped around Deke's throat, and as Longarm turned toward them, the muscles in the Ranger's arms and shoulders corded and bunched under the homespun shirt. Coffin lifted Deke off the floor and let him dangle. Deke had no choice but to let go of Coffin's gun arm and try to break the death grip.

He wasn't in time. Coffin's hand squeezed even tighter as he jerked his arm, and Longarm heard the sharp crack of Deke's neck breaking. The outlaw went limp, and when Coffin released him, Deke slumped to the floor as if every bone in his body had turned to jelly. He would never lead another raid pretending to be El Aguila.

But there was no time for the lawmen to congratulate themselves, Longarm knew. That pair of shots would bring down a storm of trouble on their heads in a matter of moments. If they were getting out of there, they had to go now.

"Head for the horses!" Longarm snapped as he stuck the pistol behind his belt.

"What are you goin' to do?" asked Coffin.

Longarm bent and hefted Sonia's body. She was still half stunned from the backhand blow. "We're taking at least one prisoner back to Texas," Longarm said grimly as he threw her over his shoulder.

That was assuming, of course, that any of them reached the border alive.

Chapter 16

Longarm heard shouts of alarm nearby as they hurried across the patio. Sonia was no lightweight, and she became even more of a handful as her wits returned to her and she began to struggle. "Stop it!" Longarm hissed at her. "Damn it, Sonia, I don't want to knock you out, but I will if I have to!"

"Bastard!" she yelped as she struck at his back with her fists. "*Amigos!* Back here! Help me!"

She was kicking her feet at the same time, and as one of them sunk into Longarm's belly and made him gasp for breath, he muttered, "The hell . . . with this!"

He stopped short, lowered the surprised Sonia, and clouted her in the jaw with a loose fist. Her head jerked to the side, and she once again slumped senseless in his arms. Longarm bent over and lifted her onto his shoulder again.

"If you're through waltzin' around with that gal, Long," called Coffin, "you'd better get mounted up." The big Ranger had already swung up into the saddle of one of the horses tied at the edge of the patio.

There was an extra mount now that Barton wouldn't be coming with them. Longarm didn't want to take the time to tie Sonia onto the saddle of the remaining horse either. He said to Coffin, "Grab the reins of those other critters. We may need extra mounts before we're through."

"That's just what I was thinkin'," said Coffin as he leaned over to jerk loose the reins from the flowering shrub where he had tied them.

Longarm saw that Coffin had brought the bay mare from the stable. With a grunt of approval, he slung Sonia's body over the back of the horse, just in front of the saddle. Holding her there awkwardly, he mounted the bay and took hold of its reins.

A group of outlaws came boiling around the corner of the house, while several more ran out the rear door. One of the men yelled orders in Spanish, while another shouted, "There they are! Don't let 'em get away!"

Longarm snapped a shot at the group on the patio while Coffin threw lead at the ones near the corner of the house. The gunfire made all of the outlaws duck back into cover. Longarm and Coffin jabbed the heels of their boots into the flanks of their mounts, and the horses leaped forward into a gallop.

Wisely, Coffin had left the rear gate open when he brought the horses from the stable. The fugitives galloped through the opening as guns began to bang behind them. The outlaws had hesitated before opening fire, obviously fearing—and rightly so—that Sonia was with Longarm and Coffin. But they were unwilling to let the two lawmen escape, even if it meant taking a chance on hitting Sonia.

Riding fast in the dark like this was a chancy proposition, but Longarm and Coffin had no choice. They circled the hacienda at breakneck speed, heading for the trail that led to the gap at the end of the valley. Longarm had his hands full keeping Sonia on the horse with one hand while trying to control the galloping animal with the other.

He was also worried about Walt Scott. The man called El Aguila had to have heard the shots from the hacienda. Scott might figure that Longarm and Coffin had already been recaptured or killed. Would he go through with the planned diversion? Even if Scott intended to carry on with the plan, he might run into some of the outlaws before he was able to set off the dynamite.

Longarm figured that he and Coffin would have to outrun the pursuit to the gap and fight their way past the guards. They couldn't count on any help from Walt Scott.

The big house fell behind them. Longarm glanced over his shoulder and saw a clump of riders coming after them. Orange fire winked from gun muzzles, and Longarm faintly heard the shots over the pounding of hooves. Coffin was a little ahead of him, the Ranger's big buckskin not being forced to carry double. Neither of the lawmen tried to return the fire from behind them. Their ammunition was limited, and they might need all of it to get through the gap up ahead.

The trail sloped steadily upward, slowing the horses even more. But it would slow down the outlaws' mounts too, Longarm thought, trying to reassure himself. Another quick look back told him that the pursuit wasn't much closer. And the gap was only a few hundred yards ahead.

They had a chance. A slim one, but still a chance.

Longarm looked at the opening between the two spires of rock and bit back a groan of dismay. Enough moonlight shone down for him to see the riders who had suddenly blocked the gap. They were coming through from the other side, he realized.

The revolutionaries! The insurrectionists who wanted to overthrow Diaz who had been coming to the hacienda tonight to meet with Barton and Sonia—that had to be who the horsemen in the gap were, Longarm thought. Now the only escape route from the valley was truly blocked.

Shots began to come from up ahead. The guards at the gap must have realized that some of the prisoners were trying to flee. They would enlist the aid of the revolutionaries, and Longarm and Coffin would be mercilessly cut down. With only a handful of bullets between them, there was no way they could fight through such overwhelming odds.

Suddenly, a bright red star seemed to fall among the horsemen blocking the opening. But it wasn't a star at all, Longarm realized. It was the burning, hissing end of a length of fuse connected to a stick of dynamite. And it hadn't fallen from the heavens, but from one of the towering cliffs beside the gap. With a blast that shook the earth and lit up the night, the dynamite went off.

As the echo of the explosion rolled away through the valley and the screams of men and horses filled the air, more of the glowing points of light fell like drops of crimson rain. Longarm and Coffin never slowed down as more blasts shattered what had been a still, peaceful night. They galloped on toward the holocaust that the passage through the mountains had become.

It had to be Walt Scott up there throwing down the dynamite, Longarm realized. He must have heard the shots from the house and changed the plan, knowing that Longarm and Coffin would be leaving in a hurry. Somehow, he had gotten up there above the gap in time to use the dynamite to blast a way through for the fugitives.

Maybe Scott had soared up there like the eagle that was his namesake, Longarm thought wildly. Right now he didn't care how Scott had managed the feat. The important thing was that once again he and Coffin had a chance to get away with Sonia.

The rain of dynamite had stopped. As Longarm and Coffin raced up the last stretch of trail leading to the opening, Longarm heard an ominous rumble. He cast a desperate glance at the twin towers of rock flanking the gap, but it was too dark to see anything. He knew that the blasts could have loosened some of the rock, and an avalanche might be about to drop tons of stone and earth into the gap. "Go! Go!" Longarm shouted at Coffin. They might have only seconds to clear the opening.

No gunfire sounded as they approached the gap. The guards and the revolutionaries were all either dead or unconscious from their wounds. Longarm and Coffin had to weave their horses around gaping holes in the ground that had been blasted out by the dynamite. Bodies were sprawled everywhere.

Longarm tried not to think about the carnage. Some of the revolutionaries probably hadn't been bad men at all, merely men who'd wanted a fairer shake from their government. But they had allied themselves with a group of bloodthirsty outlaws, and they had paid the price for that folly. Longarm certainly wouldn't have traded his own life or that of Coffin for those of the revolutionaries.

The rumbling noise grew louder as the two lawmen raced through the gap. Pebbles pelted Longarm's back, and he knew that at least part of the wall was coming down. He leaned forward, shielding Sonia as much as he could with his own body. A fist-sized chunk of rock slammed into his left shoulder and made that arm go numb. Longarm gritted his teeth against the pain and kept riding. Coffin was right in front of him.

Then, with a roar that dwarfed that of the exploding dynamite earlier, huge sections of the rock wall to the left began to turn loose and slide down into the gap. A massive cloud of dust enveloped Longarm so that he could no longer see where he was going. He knew they had to be almost out of the opening, but would they make it in time?

Fresh air whipped the choking dust away from his face, and Longarm gratefully drew in big breaths of it. He looked up as he rode, and saw stars all around him on both sides. They were out of the gap. Behind them, more rock fell, blocking the opening.

Longarm's heart thudded heavily in his chest, both from the horror of almost being crushed beneath tons of rock and from relief at the narrowness of their escape. Not only had he and Coffin made it through, but the avalanche would effectively close off the gap for quite some time, maybe forever. Any pursuers would have to either dig through the wall of fallen rock or find some other way out of the valley and take the long way around.

Either way, he and Coffin would have a good-sized lead before anyone could come after them.

Coffin slowed his horse, looked back, and let out a whoop of triumph. "We did it, Long! We did it! Those sons of bitches won't catch us now! Texas, here we come!"

A part of Longarm wanted to warn Coffin not to be so confident just yet, but he couldn't bring himself to do it. Instead he just grinned wearily as he tightened his grip on

Sonia, who was starting to stir a little. Luckily, the feeling had come back in his left arm, so he could hold on to her with it while he guided the bay with the right.

"But what about Scott?" Coffin asked abruptly, his exultant mood turning solemn. "That had to be him up yonder tossin' down that dynamite. You reckon he got away?"

Longarm shook his head. "I don't know. We may never know. But we know we wanted Sonia taken back to Texas so that his name would be cleared of those raids. That's what I intend to do."

"Me too," said Coffin with a nod. "You know, he was a mighty tricky fella, but maybe Scott wasn't so bad after all. For an owlhoot, that is."

"Maybe not," agreed Longarm.

Side by side, he and Coffin rode on into the night, heading north for Texas.

The sun blistered down on the three riders as the horses moved wearily across the flat, semi-arid landscape. It was noon of the next day, and since escaping from the outlaw stronghold the night before, Longarm and Coffin had paused for only a few minutes at a time to give the horses some rest. Longarm estimated that they had covered a little over half the distance back to the border. With any luck, they would reach Del Rio sometime that night or early the next morning.

But only if they didn't have to make a longer stop, and Longarm didn't know if that was humanly possible. He and Coffin were worn down, riding on the edge of exhaustion, and Sonia swayed groggily in the saddle where Longarm had tied her. She was only half conscious, suffering from the effects of heat, hunger, thirst, and the long ride.

There hadn't been time to gather any provisions for the trip before fleeing from the hacienda, so the fugitives had been forced to make do with the game they could catch. Longarm didn't want to waste bullets, just in case they ran into more trouble, but luckily during one of their stops, Coffin had been able to bring down a jackrabbit by pegging a rock at it. They had built a small fire, roasted the rabbit lightly, and gnawed the tough, stringy meat. Sonia had even stopped complaining and threatening for a few minutes as they ate.

A few water holes along the way had provided them with a drink, but they had no canteens to fill. It would have been a relief to be able to carry water, instead of having to hope that they would run across another spring or tank, but that wasn't the case.

Still, despite the hardships, they pushed on. Longarm figured they could suffer through for another twelve to eighteen hours without much trouble. He had gone longer than that without food and water, and he figured Coffin had too.

Sonia was another matter. The pampered existence she had led had not prepared her for a grueling trek such as this.

But she had made her own choice when she'd thrown in with Barton and they had hatched their treacherous, vicious plot. She would just have to make do as best she could until they got back to Texas.

Longarm and Coffin both checked their back trail frequently, and it was Longarm who said not long after the sun was at its zenith, "Somebody's following us."

Coffin twisted in the saddle, looked back at the plume of dust rising in the distance to the south, and cursed. "Looks like a good-sized bunch, judgin' from the dust they're kickin' up."

Longarm nodded in agreement. "They're pushing their horses fast too. They must've brought extra mounts."

"Well, so did we. The gal's the lightest, so we ought to put her on your bay. Then you can take her hoss, and I'll take the one we were goin' to put Barton on."

At the mention of Barton, Sonia perked up a little and spat some more curses at them. Longarm thought Coffin's suggestion made sense, so he reined in and dismounted, going over to Sonia's horse to untie her from the saddle. He ignored the vitriol she poured out on him. Leaving her hands tied in front of her, Longarm hauled her down from the horse and carried her over to the bay. Hoisting her into the saddle took a lot of the strength he had left.

While Longarm was doing that, Coffin switched from the

buckskin to the fourth horse, a long-legged chestnut with white stockings and a white blaze on its nose. Within moments, they were all ready to ride. Longarm held the reins of Sonia's mount while Coffin led the buckskin.

They prodded the horses into a ground-eating lope. Longarm glanced back over his shoulder fairly often, gauging the progress of the pursuers. They were still closing the gap, but not as quickly now.

"Look for a stretch of rock or hardpan," Longarm called to Coffin. "We've got to throw 'em off our trail."

The big Ranger nodded his understanding. It was still a long run to the border, and anything they could do to make it more difficult for the outlaws was worth it.

Instinct told Longarm to urge his horse into a gallop, but he suppressed that impulse. The strength and stamina for a last dash might be needed later, and it would be foolish to waste those resources now. Instead he and Coffin held their mounts at the easy gait and used their eyes to search for a stretch of ground that wouldn't take tracks.

They found one about half an hour later, where some small hills that were really little more than hummocks rose from the Mexican plains. The sandy soil thinned and soon became solid, grayish-white rock. The area was several hundred yards wide and ran as far as the lawmen could see in both directions. Longarm felt a surge of relief at the sight of the rocky ground. This was just what they needed.

He and Coffin slowed the horses to a walk. Though tracks would not show up on the rock, the shoes on the hooves of their mounts could chip the stone and leave small shiny places that the eyes of an experienced tracker might spot. The delay chafed on both men, but it was better to proceed slowly and leave fewer signs of their passing.

When they were in the center of the rocky area, they turned to the west, angling toward the far side now. Again, this cost them time, and Longarm glanced anxiously at the dust cloud marking the position of the outlaws. It was closer now. He waved Coffin toward the far side of the rock.

"We'll split up now, so they won't know which set of

tracks to follow,'' said Longarm. ''See those double hills in the distance?'' He pointed to the north.

''The ones that look like a pair of tits?'' asked Coffin.

Longarm grinned tiredly. ''Those are the ones. We'll meet there at dusk. If we haven't shown up by a quarter hour after sunset, go on without us. We'll do likewise.''

''All right,'' Coffin said with a nod. ''You takin' the gal with you?''

''Yep. That all right with you?''

Coffin leaned over in the saddle and spat. ''It damn sure is. I'd've done most anything for her back there in Del Rio if she'd wanted to play a little slap an' tickle with me. But it's funny how some folks don't look near as appealin' once you get to know 'em better.''

Her face twisted with a snarl, Sonia said, ''I would sooner lay with a snake than with you, gringo.''

''The feelin's mutual, ma'am.'' Coffin lifted a big hand in farewell as he turned the horse he was riding and the buckskin toward the edge of the rocks.

Longarm rode on for more than a mile before he and Sonia left the rocky ground behind them and headed almost due north again. The outlaws would have to search a while before they found the place where Coffin had left the rocks, and when they saw the tracks of only two horses, they would be faced with a dilemma. They would have to either split up their own party or waste more time looking for the tracks Longarm and Sonia were leaving. Either way had its advantages for the fugitives.

The odds were still against Longarm and Coffin, though. The outlaw stronghold must have had another exit, Longarm figured, just as Walt Scott had thought. They couldn't have cleared away the avalanche quickly enough to be this close behind.

Longarm began to push the horses harder now. The sun was lowering in the western sky, and he wanted to reach those twin hills before time for the rendezvous with Coffin. Splitting up temporarily had been a necessary evil, but if it came down to a fight, they would stand a better chance together than apart. Sonia rode in silence now, too tired to even complain.

The light in the sky became a harsher shade, almost like that of blood, as the sun neared the horizon. A wind whipped up from the west, and things in the distance began to blur as dust filled the air. Longarm's eyes stung from the grit. When he looked back to the south, he could no longer see the dust cloud being raised by their pursuers. The air was too full of blowing sand.

Sonia roused from her half-stupor and said bitterly, "I cannot go on! We must find a place to wait out this storm."

"I said we'd meet Coffin at those double hills," replied Longarm. "That's what we're going to do." He reined in, pausing long enough to lean over in the saddle and tear a wide strip from the bottom of Sonia's skirt. As he tied it around her head so that it covered her nose and mouth, he said, "This'll help a little."

He tied his own bandanna around his head and hunched forward in the saddle as he resumed riding. It would have been better if he could have dipped the bandanna and the piece he'd torn from Sonia's skirt in some water, so that they would more effectively block the blowing sand, but that wasn't an option. Neither was stopping or turning back.

He just hoped he was still heading in the right direction. The double hills that were his destination had vanished into the sandstorm. He could see only a few feet in front of him now. To the west, the sun was a glowing orange disc that barely touched the horizon.

Even when the ground began to slope up beneath the hooves of the horses, Longarm wasn't sure they had reached the goal. He brought his mount to a stop and looked around, feeling his heart thud a little faster as he realized that he could vaguely see the outline of two small hills looming over them. Instinct had guided him and brought him to the right place. The question remained whether or not Coffin had reached this spot too.

"Coffin!" shouted Longarm. "You here, Coffin?" He had to bellow at the top of his lungs just to hope that he might be heard over the howling of the wind. He didn't hear any answer, but that didn't really mean much. Coffin might be yelling for him, but the sound was being snatched away by the fierce, sand-laden gusts.

Despite what he had told Coffin, there was no hope of going on tonight, not until the wind died down anyway. Longarm swung down from the saddle and found a sturdy little mesquite tree where he could tie the reins. He tied Sonia's horse to the same tree and lowered her from the back of the animal. Both horses turned their rumps to the wind and ducked their heads.

Longarm led a stumbling Sonia into the narrow valley between the hills. The hill to the west acted as a windbreak of sorts, though it was too small to completely block the raging demon that the storm had become. Longarm found some rocks and sat down among them, putting his back against the largest of the boulders. That helped even more. He held Sonia close beside him, wrapped in his arms—though he made sure she couldn't reach the gun he had stuck behind his belt. Of course, by now that pistol was probably so clogged with grit that it wouldn't even fire, but Longarm didn't plan to take any chances. Even in the middle of a hellacious sandstorm, he didn't trust Sonia even a little bit.

The situation could have been worse, Longarm told himself. Wherever they were, those outlaws who had been chasing them were experiencing the same choking, blinding fury of the storm. It would stop them in their tracks, just as it had stopped Longarm and Sonia. And even though Longarm and Coffin had gone to the trouble of trying to throw the pursuers off their trail, the storm would do a much more effective job of wiping out any telltale signs of their flight. This was really just about the best thing that could have happened, Longarm thought.

Provided, of course, that he didn't choke to death or wind up buried in sand before the storm finally passed . . .

Chapter 17

"Well, if this ain't a purty sight, I don't know what is."

Longarm sat up sharply at the sound of the mocking voice, his hand going automatically to the butt of the gun at his waist. He wasn't going to need the weapon, however. He realized almost right away that the voice belonged to Lazarus Coffin, who was standing nearby, his shaggy hair and beard even more tangled than usual by the wind.

Only there was no wind now. Not only that, but the sky overhead was clear, filled with bright stars and a huge, glowing moon. The silvery light washed down over the hills where Longarm and Sonia had taken refuge from the storm.

Longarm glanced to the east and saw a thin strip of light along the horizon. Dawn was an hour or so away, he estimated. The sandstorm was finally over, but while it had still been raging, Longarm had fallen asleep and dozed through most of the night.

Beside him, Sonia was stirring around. Both she and Longarm had a thick layer of dust on their clothes, and around them were little piles of sand that had settled out of the air and formed snowlike drifts. Stiffly, Longarm unwrapped his arm from Sonia and brushed away some of the dirt before pushing himself to his feet.

"Looks like you two spent a mighty cozy night," said Coffin. He still had both horses and was holding their reins as he stood there.

"At least we got to where we were supposed to be," Longarm replied. "Where were you?"

Coffin jerked a thumb over his shoulder. "Back on the other side of the hills. I didn't have no notion you two were around here. Figured I'd wait out the storm and hook up with you again later." He grinned. "Course, from the looks of things, you might be just as glad I didn't find you."

Longarm shook his head. "We were just waiting out the storm, like you." He reached down and took hold of Sonia's arm, then helped her to her feet.

"I need some water," she croaked.

Longarm's throat was pretty dry and raspy too. "We all do," he said. "But I don't know if there's any around here. We'll just have to push on and keep looking."

Sonia groaned, but she didn't complain any more as Longarm found their horses, which had also come through the storm all right. He used a rag to clean some of the dust from the horses' nostrils, then led them around the hill.

"Where do you reckon El Aguila's bunch is?" asked Coffin as the three of them mounted up and headed north again.

"You mean Barton's bunch," Longarm said. "Walt Scott turned out to be the real El Aguila, remember?"

"Oh, yeah." Coffin shook his head. "I hope that son of a buck made it through the avalanche."

"We'll probably never know," said Longarm. "But I do too." He rubbed his jaw for a moment, then went on. "I reckon those outlaws could be most anywhere. I'm sure they had to stop too when the storm hit, but there's no telling where they were by then."

"After all that wind, our tracks'll be long gone." Coffin sounded pleased at that prospect. "We've got a good chance now, Long."

Longarm nodded. He felt good about the odds too. Sometimes, even something as brutal as that sandstorm had been could have some advantages, and he didn't intend to waste this opportunity.

They pushed on, the two lawmen and their reluctant prisoner, bound for Del Rio.

"The Rio Grande!" Coffin exclaimed as they sighted the winding, slow-moving stream late that afternoon. "Prettiest river in the world—at least when you're headin' north, it is."

At the moment, Longarm could almost agree with that sentiment. On the far side of the river, visible in the distance, lay the settlement that was their destination.

They hadn't seen any more signs of pursuit during the long day, and by now they were willing to accept the possibility that the outlaws had completely lost their trail. In less than half an hour, they would reach Del Rio, and they would be safe again at last.

That thought made Longarm glance cautiously behind him. Overconfidence was something he always tried to guard against. He wasn't going to believe this was really over until they were back in Del Rio and the truth had been exposed.

He frowned as he considered what Don Alfredo's reaction would be to the news that his daughter had been plotting against him all along. Don Alfredo had always turned a blind eye to Sonia's failings. Would he again in this case? What proof did they have, Longarm asked himself, that Sonia and Barton had really been in league with the outlaws?

It might be difficult, but he and Coffin would just have to convince Don Alfredo of the truth. It would have been easier if they could have brought Barton back with them, but things hadn't worked out that way. Longarm wondered whether Barton had tried to find some excuse for his absence from Del Rio, or if the diplomat had simply vanished into the night?

"Almost there," said Coffin as the hooves of their horses splashed into the water of the Rio Grande. "Hope I ain't jinxed us by talkin' about it."

Longarm shared that hope, even though he wasn't really a superstitious man. He kept a tight grip on the reins of Sonia's horse, not wanting her to have any chance to escape when they were this close.

They crossed the river without any trouble. No outlaws showed up at the last second to throw lead at them or block their path. As they rode up the sandy bank into Texas, Longarm breathed a sigh of relief and sleeved sweat from his forehead. A few more minutes and they would be in Del Rio.

A few more minutes in which everything could go wrong, he thought grimly.

But nothing did, and as curious and startled shouts went up from the people on the boardwalks of the town, the three of them soon rode down Del Rio's main street toward the hotel and the sheriff's office.

Word of their coming must have passed quickly from building to building, because by the time the three riders reached the hotel, a sizable group was waiting for them. Don Alfredo was in the forefront, an expression of anxiety etched on his face. He brightened a little when he saw that Sonia appeared to be all right. His assistants were with him, as was Capitan Hernandez of the *federales*. Jeffery Spooner, the military officer assigned to the American delegation, was also waiting on the front porch of the hotel, along with Barton's assistants, Quine and Markson. All of them looked nervous and troubled, instead of relieved, and that puzzled Longarm. He was glad, though, to see Sheriff Sanderson hurrying along the boardwalk toward the hotel, his left arm in a sling, but otherwise apparently recovered from the injuries he'd suffered when his office was blown up.

"Sonia!" cried Don Alfredo as he stepped down from the porch and ran forward to meet them.

"Papa!" Tears ran from Sonia's eyes as Longarm brought her horse to a stop and Don Alfredo reached up for her. "Oh, Papa, it was so awful!"

She would put on a good show, thought Longarm. He and Coffin would just have to hope that the truth could counter the lies she was sure to tell.

Guiterrez helped her down from the horse, then swung a furious glare toward Longarm and Coffin. Longarm expected him to say something about the way her hands were tied, but instead he said coldly, "I am surprised you two would come back here, Señor Long. I suppose I should be grateful for the return of my daughter, but I cannot bring myself to feel gratitude to men such as you and Señor Coffin."

Longarm rested his hands on the saddlehorn and leaned forward, easing weary muscles. "Sounds to me like you don't know the whole story, Don Alfredo," he began.

"I know enough," Guiterrez snapped. "Major!"

Spooner had his hand inside his coat. He brought it out holding a gun and pointed the weapon at Longarm and Coffin. "You men are under arrest," he said. "Drop your guns."

"Under arrest for what?" Coffin burst out. "Hell, we brought that gal back just like we said we would—even though it turned out she didn't need savin' at all. Hell, she was practically runnin' that bunch of owlhoots, and—"

"Save your breath," Don Alfredo cut in. "We know all about it, Señor Coffin. We know how you and Señor Long were in league with El Aguila all along."

"But that's crazy!" said Longarm hotly. "We killed a bunch of those outlaws when they raided the town. Would we have done that if we'd been working with them?"

"Perhaps they did not know who their real leaders were at the time." Don Alfredo fumbled with the bonds around Sonia's wrists and finally got them untied. He put an arm around her shoulders and turned to lead her into the hotel. "Come along, my dear. You need food and water and much rest after your ordeal."

Longarm and Coffin gazed bleakly after them. Longarm had expected to have some trouble convincing Don Alfredo of the truth, but obviously the Mexican diplomat had already made up his mind completely. But how could Guiterrez know anything about what had happened below the border?

"I said you're under arrest," repeated Spooner. "The charges are kidnapping and treason. Now, are you going to drop your guns or not?"

"Treason!" shouted Coffin. "What in blue blazes makes you think me and Long committed treason?"

Franklin Barton stepped out of the door of the hotel and said, "I told them all about it, Coffin."

Longarm tensed in the saddle, his heart thudding in shock

at the unexpected sight of the American diplomat, as Barton went on. "We know how you and Long conspired with El Aguila to kidnap Señorita Guiterrez and hold her for ransom. Then you did your best to kill me after I delivered the money to you. But as you can see, I'm alive!"

Barton's face was pale and his features haggard, but he was definitely alive, all right, thought Longarm. The bulge of a bandage was visible under Barton's shirt and coat. Obviously, that bullet wound hadn't been fatal after all, only messy. Barton had gotten himself patched up and then somehow reached Del Rio ahead of Longarm and Coffin. The only way that was possible, Longarm knew, was if the renegade diplomat had been able to avoid the worst of the sandstorm and push on through the night.

How Barton had gotten there didn't really matter. What was important was that he had arrived in Del Rio first and filled the heads of everyone involved with lies about how Longarm and Coffin had been working with the outlaws. And as Longarm frowned, thinking furiously, he couldn't come up with any way to disprove what Barton was saying.

Lack of proof didn't bother Coffin. The big Ranger said contemptuously, "I never heard such a load of shit in my life. If you were tellin' the truth, Barton, then why in Hades would Long and me have come back to Del Rio?"

"Because you thought I was dead," Barton replied smoothly. "You thought you could spin any cock-and-bull story you wanted to about what happened down there in Mexico, and there wouldn't be anyone to dispute you."

Longarm thought he saw a narrow opening. "What about Señorita Guiterrez?" he asked. "Wouldn't we know that she would tell the so-called truth?"

Barton sighed theatrically. "Poor Sonia. You know, of course, that she has her own reasons for concealing the full truth."

Don Alfredo stopped short on the threshold of the hotel lobby. His head turned slowly, and he regarded Barton with hostile eyes. "What did you say, Señor Barton?" he asked. "Are you implying that my daughter would lie about what happened to her?"

"I'm afraid so, Don Alfredo," Barton said solemnly. His attitude conveyed clearly his reluctance to reveal the truth to his Mexican counterpart. It was all an act, of course, Longarm thought, but Barton was good at it. Barton went on. "You see—and I truly hate to tell you this—Sonia wasn't really kidnapped. She was part of the scheme with El Aguila too."

Sonia's eyes widened in amazement. *"Dios mio!"* she exclaimed. "Why do you say such things? Have you gone mad?"

"The truth has to come out sooner or later, señorita," Barton said, still acting reluctant. He turned to Don Alfredo and continued. "You see, your daughter has fallen in with a group of revolutionaries who plan to overthrow President Diaz. The ransom money that I took to the outlaw stronghold went to them, to help fund their revolution."

That was another bald-faced lie, but Longarm understood now what Barton was trying to do. When the ransom demand had come to Don Alfredo—a demand that Barton might well have written himself and passed off as coming from the outlaws—Barton had volunteered to deliver the money. That had given him an excuse to leave Del Rio. The note he had concocted might have even specified that he was supposed to carry the ransom across the border. Then he had gone directly to the stronghold, where, thanks to Longarm, Coffin, and Walt Scott, things hadn't gone exactly as planned.

Longarm knew that the ransom money hadn't gone to the revolutionaries. Scott's rain of dynamite had prevented that. So what had happened to it?

Longarm was willing to bet that Barton still had the money and was planning to hang on to it in an attempt to recoup his losses as much as possible under the circumstances. But his admission that Sonia had been involved with the revolutionary group—which was true as far as it went—was a bold step no doubt calculated to cover Barton's trail that much more. Barton was a cunning gent. He had mixed lies, truths, and half-truths to make himself look like a hero and damn everyone else involved.

He might just get away with it too. Anything to the contrary that Longarm, Coffin, or Sonia might say would be discounted as attempts to protect themselves by lying.

Those thoughts flashed through Longarm's head as Sonia gaped in anger and astonishment at Barton. The renegade diplomat shook his head solemnly at her, as if in pity, and turned away. His eyes met Longarm's for an instant, and the marshal saw a flicker of triumph glittering there.

"Come, Sonia," Don Alfredo said coldly to his daughter as he tugged her into the lobby of the hotel. "We have much to talk about, you and I. Some things can be forgiven, but others . . ."

"But, Papa—" Sonia protested. Don Alfredo tugged on her arm, silencing her.

A few feet away on the boardwalk, Major Spooner had drawn back the hammer of his revolver, and his finger was taut on the trigger. "I won't tell you again to drop your weapons and surrender," he said to Longarm and Coffin.

"Well, then, soldier boy," grated Coffin, "I reckon you'd better go ahead and shoot me, 'cause a Ranger don't surrender."

Spooner looked at Longarm, who shook his head slowly. Billy Vail might give him hell for it later on—if there was a later on—but Longarm just wasn't in a surrendering mood either.

Suddenly, there was a flash of motion from the door of the hotel. Sonia leaped toward Major Spooner, her father lunging futilely after her. She reached out and plucked the gun from the hand of the young officer, whom she had taken completely by surprise. Longarm yelled, "No!" as Sonia spun toward Barton, who was as startled as Spooner had been.

"Liar!" shouted Sonia, the bitter accusation blending in with the sound of the shot as she jerked the trigger.

Barton's eyes widened in shock, but that was all he had time for before the bullet smacked into the side of his head, bored through his brain, and exploded out the other side of his skull in a grisly shower of blood, gray matter, and splintered bone. He swayed for a second, already dead on his feet, before he pitched to the side and thudded onto the planks of the boardwalk. Glowering at his body, Sonia lowered the still-smoking gun.

"S-Sonia . . ." her father said tentatively, reaching out to her. Other than that, a shocked silence ruled the street.

Sonia let the gun slip from her hand and fall to the boardwalk. "He was a thief," she said in a voice that was half moan. "He must have wanted to steal the money all along. He never believed in the cause!"

"Then what he said . . . what he said about you . . . it was true?" Don Alfredo's voice was as bleak as the grave, and so was the expression on his face. Sonia just looked at him in stony silence.

Sheriff Sanderson stepped forward and knelt beside Barton's body. With his uninjured arm, he searched the dead man's clothes and brought out a paper-wrapped packet from an inside pocket of Barton's coat. "Reckon he figured to take off with this as soon as he could," said the sheriff. He tossed the package to Major Spooner, who caught it instinctively. "Open that up and see what's inside it, young fella."

With trembling fingers, Spooner tore away the paper and revealed a thick stack of Mexican currency. "It's . . . the ransom money," he said in amazement. "I saw Don Alfredo hand it to Mr. Barton with my own eyes."

Don Alfredo nodded in confirmation. "*Sí*. I wired my bank in Mexico City for it and had it brought to me from the bank downriver in Cuidad Acuna." His voice shook a little. "That is nearly all the money I have in the world." He looked at Sonia, who stared back defiantly at him. "But it would have been worth it. . . ."

Another silence fell, but it lasted only a few seconds before Coffin said, "I reckon we ain't under arrest no more."

"I reckon not," Longarm agreed.

They watched as Sheriff Sanderson took hold of Sonia's arm and led her away toward the jail, which Longarm saw had had some hasty repairs made to it. Don Alfredo watched them go, standing on the boardwalk with his shoulders slumped in an air of utter defeat.

Longarm was relieved that the truth had come out and that justice had caught up with Franklin Barton when it had looked as if the man was going to get away with his treachery.

But he couldn't be completely happy with the way everything had turned out. No, sir, not by a long shot.

Chapter 18

The strains of guitar music floated through the warm night. Del Rio was quiet and peaceful once more. Maybe with any luck it would stay that way for a while, Longarm thought as he and Lazarus Coffin ambled along the boardwalk in company with Sheriff Sanderson.

"Well, after everything you've told me, Lazarus," mused Sanderson, "I don't reckon we've got to go hunt down El Aguila after all."

"Nope, he didn't have anything to do with those raids," Coffin agreed. "It was just that bunch of owlhoots usin' his name so they could set up that phony kidnappin'."

"Truth to tell, I didn't much plan on goin' after him anyway," Sanderson said as he paused and leaned on the railing along the edge of the boardwalk.

A deep voice came from the shadow-cloaked mouth of a nearby alley. "I'm glad to hear that, Sheriff."

Longarm and Coffin both turned sharply toward the alley. "Scott!" exclaimed Coffin. "Hellfire, mister, is that you?"

Longarm wasn't surprised to see the tall figure of Walt Scott move out of the darkness and step up onto the boardwalk. Scott moved easily and seemed none the worse for wear, considering the destruction he had wreaked on the way out of the stronghold in Mexico.

"Howdy, Scott," said Longarm. "I didn't figure we'd ever see you again. You must've scooted pretty fast to get away from that avalanche."

"I had to light a shuck, all right," Scott agreed dryly. "But I got off the rim in time and worked my way back down to where I'd left Phantom. I thought maybe I could catch up to you boys before you got to the border, but I ran into this sandstorm that had other ideas."

"Yeah, it slowed us down too," said Coffin. "How come you changed the plan we had and headed for the gap with that dynamite, instead of the other end of the valley?"

Longarm had wondered about that himself. He wasn't surprised when Scott said, "I overheard a couple of those owlhoots talking about how the guards at the gap had signaled down that those revolutionaries were about to enter the valley. I knew that would block your path for sure, so I went that direction instead of the other way and found a place where I could climb up above the opening."

Coffin snorted in disbelief. "I looked at them cliffs. They looked mighty sheer to me."

"I didn't say it was an easy climb," Scott said with a chuckle as he took the makin's from his shirt pocket and began to roll a quirly.

Longarm took advantage of the opportunity to light up a cheroot, then blew out a lungful of smoke and said, "I guess considering everything, Coffin and I can forgive you for lying to us and acting like you were double-crossing us in that cantina."

"I appreciate that," said Scott. "But I've got to admit, Marshal, I probably lied to you more than once."

Sanderson grinned at the tall drifter. "Goin' to tell 'em the truth, Walt?" he asked.

Longarm frowned. "You two know each other?"

"Most of the star-packers in the border country know El Aguila," said Sanderson. "We've all heard tell that he's an outlaw—but we know not to believe everything we hear."

Scott's long fingers went to the broad leather belt around

his waist and plucked something from a hidden pocket behind it. As he held out his hand, the light from a nearby window gleamed for a second on the thing that lay in his palm.

It was a silver star in a silver circle—the emblem of the Texas Rangers.

"Son of a bitch!" Coffin said. "You mean you're really a Ranger, instead of an owlhoot?"

Scott stowed the badge away with a deft motion. "It comes in mighty handy sometimes for folks to believe that I'm crooked," he said. "But Captain McNelty and Major Jones know the truth, and now so do you."

Coffin shook his head. "I won't say nothin', Scott. You got my word on that."

Longarm grinned around the cheroot in his mouth. "My memory's getting plumb bad, Scott. I've already forgotten anything I just saw."

"Thanks," Scott said. He let out a low whistle, and the big black stallion emerged from the alley and came over beside the boardwalk. Scott swung up into the saddle and continued. "I'd better be riding. I've got word that there's another little dustup brewing over in the Big Bend. Thought I'd go take a look, see if maybe I ought to play a hand or two." He sketched a quick salute to the brim of his hat, then turned the stallion and rode away, vanishing into the night.

"Well, hell," said Coffin with a sigh, "if that don't beat all." His attitude brightened. "I think I'm goin' to hunt up Anna Marie. I ain't seen her since we got back." He glanced over ominously at Longarm. "Unless you want to fight me again over her."

Longarm shook his head. "No, you go right ahead, Coffin. I've got a word of advice for you, though."

"What?" Coffin asked suspiciously.

"Try being nice to her for a change, instead of acting like a big ol' bull. You might be surprised how she responds."

"You reckon?" Coffin frowned skeptically. "I 'spose I can try it, but it ain't really my style." He ambled off down the boardwalk toward Kilroy's.

When Coffin was gone, Sanderson looked curiously at

Longarm and said, "That surprises me a mite. I didn't figure you for the type to give up a gal to another fella like that and even tell him how he ought to court her."

"Well," said Longarm with a grin, "a gent don't always have to wind up with the girl, now does he?"